Virginia

Also by R. Bertematti

Project Death

The Undead: First of The Desposyni Chronicles*

*published by Tridium Press

Virginia

A Romance of the Civil War

R. Bertematti

Who can conceive, who has not proved,
The anguish of a last embrace?
When, torn from all you fondly loved,
You bid a long adieu to peace.
                    —*Byron, To Emma*

Tridium Press

ISBN: 978-0-578-00220-0

Printed in the United States of America by Tridium Press

For my mother and father

Contents

Note

It has been now over two score years since the extraordinary events of this narrative transpired, and the drums of war have thankfully long ceased their dire sound. I write now in the twilight of my days, an old merchant and soldier, while my mind still breathes with memories. Let the reader be assured that these are not fanciful tales, nor that my story is the product of a senile mind: I have tried to recollect, with care and accuracy, a part of what occurred to me so long ago.

At such a time my eyes fell upon a member of that despised race, for whose cause our nation shed much blood. It was her love that, in my darkest moments, gave me life; and through these long years, whilst my limbs have grown weak and my eyes become dim, that same love has never ceased to sustain me. To her, and to the loving memory of my first wife, I devote this work.

S. Roget

Inwood-on-the-Hudson, New York, 1909

ONE

A CURIOUS REQUEST

The cemetery, as always in the late, waning afternoon, was still and quiet. I stood alone among the vast hordes of the dead. But of all the alabaster monuments, in row upon row, as far as my eyes could see, I doted only over one—that of my dear wife Madeline, who had passed from this world whilst it was yet gripped in Spring, as a flower, at once fair blooming, quickly perishes. It was the day before departing on the journey this narrative will relate, and I went to bid farewell to the light that illumined my life for twelve happy years, but which was cruelly extinguished, leaving me in a contemptible darkness.

Her mound was already well covered with grass. I had witnessed the growth progress from a few blades out of the brown loose earth to a lush carpet. What an irony that though my wife lay underneath, the top, for all to see, grew verdant with life. That grass was a part of her: the final reminder of her bodily existence, for I could point to it and say—See! Her very flesh is the nourishment and fodder of it;—but Whitman stated it better than I.

As I stood meditating on the foregone joys of our life together, and the sorrows of my present life alone, the sudden grinding of wheels upon gravel startled me. I turned to see a cart stop not far from me. The old driver removed his cap and waved it in the air calling : "Hullo, sir!—we're closing now! Do you hear, sir?" I lingered for another moment with my love, then bade farewell and followed the path out through the great iron gates. It did not take long to hire a cab, and I took my seat therein across from a man who felt obliged to move his walking stick off the seat I came to utilize. We exchanged greetings; but I, not desirous of further converse, turned to look out of the window. The man presently withdrew a folded newspaper from under his arm and splayed it on his lap.

"I'd say a few more weeks now," said he, "and we'll have an all out war."

I glanced at the newspaper. There was an item about President Lincoln proclaiming a blockade of southern ports.

"They'll take the yard in Norfolk," he continued. "I know they will. When that happens, all hell will break loose. First Sumter, and then all hell."

Without another word, for which I was thankful, the man folded his paper, tapped his walking stick against the ceiling of the cab, and left me alone to continue home.

Not far from the village, at about two miles, rested a little valley surrounded by high hills. I possessed a modest home in its quietest corner, nestled among tall walnut-trees. Only two lights shone within as I reached it: one in the kitchen and another in the dining room,—both windows bright and beckoning against the darkness descending on the valley.

The front door opened ere I reached it, and my small daughter ran out to embrace me as she was wont to do at my late arrivals. I walked into the house with her sitting on my neck, and with my brows covered by her miniscule hands. My old negro Frederick came to remove my little bundle.

"She'll catch her death in cold, someday, I tell her," he said in his peculiar mumbling fashion, due to lack of teeth, as he placed Andrea on her seat at the dinner table.

"How are you, Frederick?" I inquired.

"Well, sir; and yourself?" asked he, helping me with my coat.

"Well and thankful," said I.

"Hello, Poppa," said my eldest daughter Madeline from her place at the table. I went to her and kissed her, holding her tender face in my hands as I admired, not for the first time, the resemblance to her namesake.

"Set yourself, sir, and I'll get supper," said Frederick. He left and returned from the kitchen with several trays somehow balanced in his thin arms. I sat between my daughters, they at each end, and assisted him in setting the table.

"Are you truly going to-morrow, Poppa?" asked Madeline.

"Yes: early to-morrow."

"How long will you be?"

"Several weeks, I am sure.

"Will you miss us?"

"Very much."

"You think Grampie will be well?"

"I hope so," said I, but not without the proper amount of empathy.

My daughters had never seen their grandfather in the flesh; even I—his son—
had seen him last while still a boy, when he separated from my mother and
headed South to make his fortune. And yet, I had strangely cultivated in my
children's hearts the idea they had a relative dear and to be cherished. Grampie
never failed to send them gifts at Christmas-time, and through that act alone
secured an immortal and esteemed place in their universe.

"You're going to take a steam-boat, Poppa?" asked Andrea.

"Yes; a big, old steamer."

"I wish I could go with you."

"What about your schoolwork?"

"You're only in your first lessons, too!" her older sister chided.

"We'll all go together some day," said I to palliate them. The
proposition so pleased them that they smiled triumphantly at one another.

After supper I sent little Andrea and Madeline each to their rooms
with a kiss on the forehead. I remained at the table until Frederick reappeared
to clear it.

"Sit down," said I, and poured him a glass from the nearly empty wine
bottle. Frederick sat down across from me in the chair where my Madeline
would sit.

"You have been with the family a long time," I observed.

"Yes, sir; I served the late missus' father."

"Take a drink, please."

The old negro took the glass in his ashen, bony hands, and with his
eyes shut took a mouthful of the liquid.

"May I say something, sir?"

"What is it?"

"You've taken to drinking a lot of wine lately, sir."

I glanced at the bit of wine left in the bottle. Frederick only contemplated me with his large, yellowed eyes. After a moment of reflection I left my seat and walked about the room until I came to a photograph of my wife on the wall. Madeline looked askance and far away in the sepia-colored oval portrait. "I know," I finally responded.

"I watched the late missus grow up into a fine lady, sir. But the Lord was pleased to take her to his kingdom. I know she watches over you and over the children; and if she could come down and talk to you, she would tell you that it ain't good for a man to be alone, just like the Scriptures say. Yes, sir, a man always needs a woman, especially if there are children that need minding. I'm an old man, sir, and I don't know how much longer I can be of service to you, though it's my pleasure to do so.

"What I want to say, sir, is that you should find yourself a lady— though none, I know, will ever be as fine as the late missus—to marry who'll be a good mother to these children because an old man like me can do his best, but a mother he'll never be."

I returned to the table and sat. "It's been a year."

"A bit more than that, sir."

"It has felt like an eternity. I stayed by her side to the end, hoping the sickness would leave her and come to me. Who would ever think, Frederick, that a woman like her would die so young? She was so strong, so ruddy, so full of health and vigor!"

I felt my eyes begin to water, and, not wanting Frederick to see my frailty, covered them with my hand. My other hand, resting on the table, I felt Frederick cover with his own. I wanted to reach down and kiss the hand of so faithful and compassionate a fellow! When I composed myself and looked at him, he pulled his hand back as if guilty of some terrible breach of formality.

"I want to be out around four on the morrow," said I, heading toward the staircase.

"Everything will be ready for you, sir," I heard Frederick say.

Reaching my chamber, I removed my shoes and lay down on the bed. From my pocket I removed the letter I had received a fortnight past. By the light of the lamp beside me I read it again:

Saint Odile Sanatorium
New Orleans, Louisiana
March 23rd, 1861

Dear Mr. Roget—

It is our regret to inform you that your father, Mr. Alistair Roget, has been admitted to our facility for treatment of severe lung paroxysms. On the 12th he collapsed in his home. Until now his condition has been stable, but we fear it will not improve.

Mr. Roget has requested that you come to see him as soon as permissible. Enclosed you will find several bank notes which he entrusted us to send for the expenses of your journey.

Yours most truly, &c,
Dr. Martin Penaud

I was on the eve of departing, and what awaited me south in that port city I could not then imagine. We were almost in an inevitable war, and here I was like some Dante headed into the heart of the furnace. My father had to be seriously ill to ask to see me, a request never existent all the long years he was well.

TWO

MY JOURNEY COMMENCES

Early the next morning, while it was yet dark, at a point where my dreams were sufficiently entertaining so as to absolve me of all worries, Frederick came to awaken me and help me dress. The carriage outside was ready and loaded with my baggage. I patted him on the shoulder as he bade me a good journey. Thanks I gave him and asked him to make sure my girls continued faithfully in their schoolwork, particularly Andrea, in whom I was never able to instill the love of studies. He promised to fulfill his duty and saw me off. As we went down the road I looked back until my bower dwindled into the dark woods.

At dawn, or shortly afterward, I boarded a train on the first leg of my journey. Three days later I arrived in Saint Louis where I transferred to a large steam boat, *Le Siecle*, and began my trip down the truly mighty Mississippi.

Each evening, I took the pleasure of sitting on the bow deck along with several of the other passengers, enjoying the warm, humid breeze. Occasionally we would pass the lights of a small town or settlement along the banks of the river. Invariably the ship would then be accosted by a horde of rafts and canoes as it passed, to the delight of the passengers, who threw down coins, particularly if our curious visitors were children. I found myself often at the railing, perhaps contributing some coins, but soon grew tired of the attraction and passed on my opportunity to greet the natives.

The last evening on the water found me on the open deck enjoying a glass of wine. There I fell asleep but was soon awakened by the excited cries of the passengers, standing and looking fore. I made my way forward for a view and witnessed developing before me a great expanse of colored lights, which grew and grew until we were swallowed by them.

The steam boat docked at a long wharf where jumping and shouting children outnumbered adults. The ramp to the wharf was lowered and the captain himself, whom I had seen once or twice, debarked first. We all filed down the ramp behind him. The captain and his stewards kindly held the hands of the women as they passed onto the wharf. There were many negroes walking about, laden with bags. A large one, dressed in white shirt and pantaloons, but shoeless, approached me and bowed slightly.

"Sah, dese permentoes is yours?" he asked.

"Those are mine."

"Gil at yer savice, sah."

"Take me to a hotel, please."

"A hotel it is, sah."

He, a foot and a half taller than I, took up my bags and I followed. We walked off the wharf and merged with the other persons into the avenue.

"Did de boat treet yah good?" he asked me.

"It was fine."

"Eber been in dis ol' city?"

"No, this is my first time South."

"Yah done sey!"

"You work as a porter?" I asked out of curiosity.

"Nah, sah. I b'long to massah Culpepper. He les me go out in de night ta make some mo' money by carr'ing dese bags fo' folk."

"You're a slave, then?"

"Yes, sah."

While I walked beside the negro, I looked up often at his earth-black face to find him smiling. When he spoke he did not look at me, but only straight ahead. Harriet Stowe's excellent treatment of slave life came to mind (a very moving work) which I along with practically everyone else had read, and here I was walking beside a member of her *dramatis personae*. How different this man seemed to me from my Frederick, though springing from the same maternal stock and ancestral heritage. Frederick was educated and spoke well, his attitudes and manners similar to mine or any other man's, his physical form developed clearly within the environs of a city. But this man was large and muscular, the product of the rawest of foodstuffs and hard labor on the land, rude and contemptible, his manners deficient of even the minimum to function in a white society. He seemed perfectly adapted only for hard labor.

"Dere, sah—dere's a good place fo' yah," said he as we ascended the porch of a tall, yellow building with several rows of balconies adorned with dangling vines. I inquired about a room and was directed upstairs, the negro following me with my bags. I walked into the room, and he lay my bags just inside the door, but did not cross the threshold.

"Dere yah go, sah." he said.

"Thank you."

"Can Gil do aintin' else for yah, sah?"

I inquired if he knew where the hospital at which my father was confined was located. He concentrated as he thought.

"Nah, sah. De genelman at de desk nose fo' shur."

I handed the negro some coins, at which amount he was very pleased, and thanked him again for his service. He bowed slightly and left me, shutting the door behind him.

The toilet contained a tub of cool water awaiting me, as well as bottles of fragrant soaps more of use to a woman, but for which I was thankful after more than a week of travel. After removing my clothing, I bathed and then dressed myself in a new suit I had purchased for the journey.

Before departing to find my father, I stood outside on the balcony and looked out over the city.   As yet I had not seen the elegance I expected of New Orleans, except for the gaily dressed men and women who filled the streets. In the distance, the moonlight reflected in shimmering streaks on the bayou waterways where lights were scattered and went on and off like lightning bugs in a dark wood.

The proprietor of the hotel identified the hospital as being in the *Vieux Carre*, or the French Quarter of the city. His own son, a boy of twelve, ran out to find me a carriage while I waited on the porch, leaning against a column. The carriage appeared promptly and conveyed me through the city and into the French Quarter. At last I began to see the Old World in the New. The houses now appeared magnificently opulent, large and sturdy, influenced by Spanish and French building styles, with well manicured lawns and colorful gardens overflowing with the gayest varieties of flowers. How I wished that it was daylight in order to take in more of that architectural luxury, since my weak vision was ill-accustomed to the night. I could hear music from various parts, a curious but pleasant syncopated rhythm arising from brass instruments. The sights and sounds would not have been complete without stimulus to that third important sense, well provided for by various bakeries—or *patisseries,*—we passed, redolent with breads and pastries of all kinds. For a moment it seemed I forgot the true object of my visit to this little France, for when the carriage halted before the hospital, I wondered why we had stopped.

The hospital was a wide, low building of white stone with a statue of Saint Odile in a small flower garden before it. I sat waiting for a half-hour until a small, quick man with moustaches and spectacles—Dr. Penaud, the physician who had written me—appeared to shake my hand and to lead me to his office. Though his manner when greeting me was neither grave nor jovial, I knew at once what news he planned to give me concerning my father. I followed him quietly until we were seated in his office and he had shut the door.

"I trust you had a pleasant trip here, Mr. Roget," he said with not a trace of an accent, to my surprise, because the Gallic ancestry of his face was obvious.

"It went well, thank you," I responded.

"Did you receive my second letter?"

"No," I said: "only the one which summoned me here."

"Well, with deep regret I must tell you that Mr. Roget, your father, passed away ten days ago."

Perhaps my unaffected manner unnerved him, because he sat rigid, expecting me to say or do something. But truly, the news, though I guessed what it was to be (and even had I not) moved me as little as if the doctor had informed me of the death of a stranger.

"How did he die?"

"In his sleep."

"Did he leave any message for me?"

The doctor let escape a chuckle which he quickly waved away as an act not appropriate to the circumstances.

"You were not close to your father?"

"No. I had not seen him in sixteen years."

"You know that he was a wealthy man?"

"I surmised such."

"Well," the doctor said, "he left you a large part of his estate, including, I believe, his plantation."

"Are you certain?"

"His lawyers will be here to-morrow and they will explain everything to you. I beg your pardon: I only knew of his medical condition and nothing else."

"Are you certain we are talking of the same man?"

"You are Stanton Roget, are you not?"

"Yes."

"Indeed we are."

I left the hospital and returned to the hotel. On my bed I lay and fantasized about my situation. I had done well for myself in New York, building a trading business out of nothing, but I never considered myself wealthy despite my copious reserves. If the doctor was correct, then I had been suddenly and unexpectedly plunged into Southern aristocracy. What was

I to do with a plantation? A plantation contained slaves, and though I considered the negro inferior in many ways to the white man, slavery was abhorrent to me as a condition unfit for any man regardless of his race. What was I to do with slaves? And was not my father remarried? What of his wife? These questions I tossed around in my head for several long hours before I could fall asleep.

THREE

MY INHERITANCE DISCLOSED

The lawyers, Misters McLee and McLee, happened to be brothers who looked not at all alike except for their girths. From their rotundity, I guessed that they did very well at their profession.

The doctor, the two lawyers, and I, sat around a table in a small meeting room. Where I sat, the sun fell directly on me through a large window and made me feel very hot. A nurse brought us all tall glasses of ice water. The lawyers each had a neat pile of documents before them.

"Our firm," one of them began, "McLee, McLee, and Finlay, have worked with the late Mr. Alistair Roget for some time in supervising business and personal arrangements of all sorts. Consequently, he prepared his last will and testament to be carried out after his death, by us, exactly according to his instructions."

"The late Mr. Roget," the other continued as the first ended, as if on a cue, "designated you, Mr. Stanton Roget, his son by a previous marriage, to be the inheritor of his estate and his sugar cultivation enterprise. As you can see by this sealed and signed document, you are the designated heir."

I took the document that he handed me and looked over it. Indeed, my name was there in bold calligraphy.

"The estate of the late Mr. Roget," continued the first McLee, "is composed of a plantation house at four— dollars; one hundred and twenty-five acres of land appraised at six— dollars; fertile soil on that land yielding an average crop of ten— pounds of sugar per season, yielding a revenue of eighteen— dollars per annum; fifty-two slaves, eighteen of them children below the age of thirteen, with a combined market value of twelve— dollars; an undisclosed amount held by three banks; and an interest in a shipping business which, at his instruction, we sold for a profit of two— dollars."

He read me the net worth of the inheritance, and I was very surprised at how well my father had done for himself. And now it was mine! Any other man would have been in ecstasy at being left such a great amount of wealth, but I must admit that I received the information quite calmly and without even a glint of the love of lucre in my eye. Perhaps I did not appreciate how comparable a wealth derived from a rural economy was to the urban enterprises to which I had devoted my life. The documents detailing the various holdings of my father I took several minutes to examine, as well as the deeds to each of the fifty-two slaves.

"Did my father inform you why I was designated his principal heir?" I asked, curious about the position of his current wife and children.

"Your father," the second McLee said, "knew of your successful textile trading business in New York. It was evident to him that none other of his extant family possessed the know-how to continue the plantation business and to manage the finances."

"But I know nothing about cultivation!" I observed.

"By the late Mr. Roget's admission, neither did he when he first began this enterprise. His lands have always been in the care of a freedman, Antoine Chevaux. Mr. Chevaux continues his duties and awaits you as his new employer."

"What of his wife and children?"

"In essence, you have inherited them also."

I had lost my wife, a cherished member of my household, the delight of my eyes—and here I had acquired a whole family! Did my father think he was doing me a service by this gift?

"Where is the plantation?" I asked.

"It is two miles south of here. We can go there now if you'd like."

I agreed to go view this Trojan horse after lunch. We met again in front of the hospital, though the doctor was no longer part of our company. We rode a carriage out of the city and along the alluvial plains bordering the Mississippi, passing by several marvelous plantations, with their grand old mansions in the distance. I counted myself fortunate to have seen anything, since my chubby attorneys enveloped me like a sandwich. By and by, upon passing some interesting landmark, it was pointed out to me, and I graciously displayed curiosity without knowing where was the object of interest because of my disadvantaged position.

We turned eastward, and then I was able to see through the front window of the carriage, between the legs of the driver and over the bobbing heads of the two horses, a large field of tall cane, and in the midst of it, a blue house surrounded by several dull-colored buildings. We turned toward the house and came to the grassy clearing where it stood; it had a wide porch and columns supporting a triangular roof with a large, round window in the center, like the eye of some cyclops. An old negress sat on a chair on the porch, and several negro children played before the house. The oldest of them ran toward us and settled the horses as our carriage made a stop. I was relieved to step out of my constrained position. As soon as the lad saw me, he yelled "He here!" back toward the house. The old woman left her chair and went inside. The older children ceased their play and stood up all together with their hands behind their backs. The younger ones were undeterred and continued their games. The lawyers stood to either side of me, and it seemed we stood there a long while. By and by the front door of the house opened and a woman appeared. The old negress came up behind her, opening a parasol, and held it over her. Together they walked off the porch and came toward me. The woman seemed young, perhaps my age, and had blond hair tied with ribbons above her head, so that it poured down like a mane about her neck. She wore a simple black dress with a beige cummerbund about her waist. The closer she came, the more doubtful I became about what I should do or say.

"You must be Mr. Stanton Roget?" she asked.

"Yes," said I.

"This is Madam Beatrice Roget," the first McLee introduced me.

"It is a pleasure, madam," said I, kissing her extended hand. "Please allow me to express my sincerest condolences at your loss."

"Thank you," said she; "we share, then, a mutual sorrow."

She led us into the house and to the sitting-parlor, where we sat on couches covered with white silk pillows. The negress brought us lemonade and cookies. The lawyers took their customary positions to either side of me, and the negress sat on a stool by her mistress.

For an half-hour my companions repeated to Mrs. Roget and I much that I had heard at the hospital, in addition to more details about the estate and the last wishes of the elder Roget. Mrs. Roget was to receive a generous monthly stipend and would retain deed to the house and land in the event of my death.

It was then decided that I should meet the overseer, Mr. Antoine Chevaux. The old negress sent the boy who had tended to the horses to find the gentleman. In the meantime, while waiting, I inquired concerning the children and was told there was one adolescent boy and one girl of twelve years of age. They were still at school and would not return for several hours still. I was tempted to ask Mrs. Roget her age, but thought better of it; she must have been a young woman when she wed my father.

Presently a tall, handsome, square-jawed mulatto, Mr. Chevaux, entered and stood before me in tall riding boots and a vest of leather. His grip in handshake was powerful.

"Mr. Chevaux is a freedman. He oversees the slaves," Mrs. Roget informed me.

"At your service, *monsieur*," he said to me without a trace of the smile of geniality. "Would you like a tour of the plantation now?"

I glanced at the lawyers and shook my head. "No, I think I shall postpone it until to-morrow. I am still rather weary from my journey."

"To-morrow, then, *monsieur*," Mr. Chevaux said, turned curtly, and walked out.

"Will you stay for supper?" Mrs. Roget asked.

"No," I replied, truly tired and wishing to return to my hotel. Or perhaps my weariness was more a mental one than a physical. "I think I shall go. I promise to return to-morrow."

"Very well, Mr. Roget," said the mistress and saw us out. Within the carriage, the lawyers and I assumed our familiar positions, which I detected seemed to give them some pleasure. At a slow gallop, no doubt because of the weight the horses had to pull, we left behind the house and the sugar cane and returned to the city.

At my hotel room, the two lawyers presented me with all pertinent documents, and with an envelope from the bank containing a great amount of notes. They informed me of the location of their offices, and instructed me to visit them within the week to inform them of the status of my new situation. I declined their offer to accompany me again the next day, saying that I was able to manage on my own. When they finally left me, I piled all of the documents on one side of the bed and I lay on the other in an attempt, within a restful repose, to decide what I was to do. But a restlessness stirred me to get up and to compose a letter to Frederick detailing precisely all that was occurring. My business back home was in capable hands, but I could not leave it indefinitely. Even more importantly, I had my daughters to look after, and did not wish to be too long away from them.

What I would have given to have my Madeline there with me again! It is pitiful how life allows one to have a bite of the most delectable happiness, and then snatches it away like the cruel judge of Tantalus. No woman ever possessed a more wise and level head. Together we could iron out every difficulty. One touch of her gentle hand would settle my distresses, and an encouraging word from her was worth more to me than the counsel of a hundred friends. Man, despite his apparent superior position in society, is as incapable and helpless as a new born babe. He must go from woman to woman, from mother to wife, and always must be subject to her careful guidance and to the nurturing comfort of her feminine virtues. She is the rudder of his ship, the bit to his horse, the spark that keeps the fire of life in his bosom burning. Without a woman, at whatever stage, a man is as impotent as our father Adam the morning of the sixth day when he searched vainly among the beasts for a helpmeet. And it took the compassion of the Lord to build a mate of very him. Madeline was part of me, and when she perished that part perished also.

FOUR

A NEW ACQUAINTANCE

The next morning, I was early awakened by the shouts of some commotion outside my window. But when I reached the balcony to determine what was the matter, the dispute, wherever it was, had apparently ended because I saw nothing of importance. I was thankful for the apparent fracas, however, for it had prevented me from oversleeping.

It being a sunny and pleasant morning, I went out for a walk after deciding that I would leave the trip back to the plantation until the afternoon. So I ambulated, admiring the local establishments and the beautiful dresses of the matrons who walked about, until I reached a large commons, a marketplace, where foodstuffs were sold. There, a noisy crowd by a building attracted my attention. From where I stood, I could not see very clearly what was the object of the gathering, and so out of curiosity I made my way there. It was a large crowd of men, most wearing derbies and top-hats despite the heat of the day, making me conjecture they were business-men of some sort. They were gathered around a low wooden platform, like a stage, under the boughs of a young tree. Upon the stage stood a well-dressed man, with a long, overcast face, wildly moving a horse stick in one hand and in the other a cluster of sheets of paper. On the ground in front of the stage sat several negroes. As I came closer and made my way into the throng, I could more clearly see their faces; they seemed to me the most profoundly saddened faces I had ever seen on negroes. Gone were the jovial looks and the white teeth to which I was so accustomed. They sat on the ground with their legs crossed, men and women, looking up at the crowd of men. One had his arm around a woman who was holding a small child between her legs; the child was playing with the grass, ripping it out of the ground, and with it decorating the hair of its mother.

Sitting among the negroes was a young woman that caused me to look twice before I focused my attention on the actions of the man upon the stage. She appeared the lightest of the negroes, with fine features that contradicted her ancestry. She seemed a mulatto, perhaps even a quadroon. Her dress was colored orange, and patterned with purple blossoms, the collar unlaced, revealing a long and graceful neck. Though my eyesight was not the best, and even at short distances I could not perceive fine detail, it was clear to me that this poor girl was an exquisite creature. Her skin had not a flaw on it— smooth, of a vivid saffron-color. Her hair was auburn, long and curly, held at the neck by a rag the same color as her dress. She sat with her knees against her chest, with her back to the wooden stage. She did not look up at the men like the others, but kept her gaze fixed on the ground before her. As I moved closer I could see that she held her lower lip in her teeth, as if ready to weep.

My attention was drawn to the auctioneer, who pointed at one of the negroes with his horse stick. Another man I had not noticed appeared, pulled the negro up, and pushed him onto the platform. The trader held the negro's forearm as he read from one of the documents he held, stating his name, age, weight, former owner, and specialty of labor. He directed the poor man to remove his frock so that all could examine his physique, which was quite delineated. When the specimen turned around, I could see faded welts across his back.

The bidding began and went back and forth for several minutes until the trader and one of the men settled on a price. The new owner came forward and climbed on the stage to examine his purchase more closely. He checked the slave's hands and then his teeth, making him open his mouth and searching there with a gloved hand. Satisfied, he stepped off the platform and the slave followed. They went through the crowd and into an adjacent building.

Next, the family with the child were put on the platform. The father and mother stood by each other holding hands. The child crawled around the platform and accepted pats on his head from several of the men. This bidding went on for a long time because no one seemed to want the whole family except an old gentleman who held at a price and would go no further. But the trader determined that he could receive a higher earning by selling the members separately, and called out leisurely for counter-offers. The crowd remained silent and not a bid was shouted. The trader then asked how much someone was willing to give for the man alone, stout and fit for labor. At once the crowd grew excited and the bidding again resumed. The old gentleman, disgusted at being thwarted at his somewhat benevolent scheme, turned and went away.

The wife picked up the child and moved closer to her mate, who embraced them both in his arms. The trader tried to pull the man toward him, but they all held together in one bundle. Several strong men jumped upon the stage and forcefully separated the man. The woman began crying out, and the child, affected by the commotion, also began to cry. The negro seemed unaffected. His face was as expressionless as that of a statue as his arms were held securely by the two men beside him. The woman and the child were pulled down to the ground, in screams. So great was her noise that one of the men struck her. At this the negro gave a howl and rushed forward, but was held back by the men. The other slaves upon the ground enveloped the woman and her child, and comforted her in her sorrow.

I was very moved by this tragic spectacle. Never had I felt the condition of slavery to be fit for any man, not even the negro. How men could unremorsefully engage in the trade of such evidently human figures I could not imagine. Were not those real tears that were shed, or merely some baseless fluid? Did not those cries of agony arise from a heart tender and cognizant of even the simplest of human emotions? I say, give me the company of a negro first before communion with these men wealthy in goods but indigent in moral decency and compassion.

Disgustedly I watched as the wife was also sold, and taken away with great noise. Only the child was left, weeping and standing alone by the trader, his small form dwarfed by the man beside him. The child stood with his hand against his mouth, his spittle falling on his frock. What a piteous sight it was when the purchase was made, and the purchaser took the child, raised its frock, and inspected its parts there in front of all. Satisfied, and with plangent child, he walked away.

I decided that I had seen enough and so turned to leave, excusing myself through the crowd, when men began to whistle and holler. To see why, I turned to see that the beautiful mulatto woman was next to be sold. My heart began to grieve, and tempted I was to leave this human market and return to my hotel. But I could not leave. I returned to my former position, prepared for another spectacle.

The men were excited, removing their hats to wave them in the air, and whistling through their fingers. I sympathized with their excitement because, though she stood humbly and without pretense, she seemed in form like an ebony Venus De' Medici, rivaling even the accepted icons of Western beauty.

"Here we have Virginia," the trader began, "age twenty-four, formerly belonging to Mr. Cassius Pickney of Laurel, Mississippi. As you can see, she's not a working nigger, but she could make a fine domestic for one of your wives. She can clean good and cook good and sew, even making this dress she's wearing. Seeing the fine condition she's in, I'll start at 4—."

The price was the highest yet since I had been there. Some bid her up while others yelled: "Let's see 'er! Let's see what she has!" The trader raised the woman's face by a finger to her chin, turning it side to side. Her price had augmented by a hundred dollars in that short time, and now the crowd grew silent. Then, with the same hand that upheld her chin, he pulled the woman's dress down from her shoulders, nearly exposing her bosom. The woman tried covering herself with her hands, but the trader pulled her hands away.

"How about now?" he asked.

At this the shouting recommenced and a steady stream of bids poured from the crowd. I had had the feeling that such an indecency was to be performed on her. My anger grew as I found myself staring at the woman; consequently I looked away, not wishing to add my eyes to her defilement. I wished to run away, far from the midst of that moral chasm.

One tall bearded man upped the price substantially. The crowd went silent. It went once. My heart was grieving, and I could feel my palms wet with a concerned excitement. It went twice.

"Hold," the bearded man said, "let me see her."

The trader looked at the man and then at the woman. He reached out his hand and held the torn dress at her waist, ready to pull it down completely.

I called out the price and then added a hundred dollars to it.

The bearded man looked at me, greatly annoyed. All heads were turned in my direction. The trader released his hold on the woman's dress, removed a handkerchief from his pocket, and wiped his forehead.

"Do I hear more?" he asked. I stood ready to match any price. It went once. It went twice. No one matched me, not even the bearded man.

"Sold to the gentleman there."

I, trembling under my clothes, stepped forward and climbed atop the platform to stand before Virginia. She kept her head lowered and did not meet my gaze. I allowed her to pull up her dress around her shoulders and lace her front. The silence was deafening and I felt like an unnerved actor in a stage drama vainly trying to remember what he is supposed to do or say.

The crowd made a passage for us and I passed through the midst of them and out of that Egypt. Once, I looked behind to see Virginia pick up her satchel from a pile. Soon we were both in the adjacent building where I offered my credentials to a clerk, signed the notes and the deed as well as other documents; all the while she sat on the window sill, quietly with her bag by her bare feet.

Having finalized the purchase, I stepped out of the building and walked away, looking behind me occasionally to see her following. When I realized fully what I had done, I stopped. *I had purchased a slave.* My purpose in doing so became so confused that I doubted the validity of my actions. If my intention had been to become a savior, then I should have acquired all of the slaves in order to set them free. Why only this colored belle?

I waited until Virginia caught up to me. As soon as she did, I reached down to help her with her bundle. She yielded her satchel to me but kept her gaze lowered, and remained silent. I knew now that my weak eyes had not deceived me with their usual habit of glossing over imperfection and detail when beholding a thing at a distance. This choice specimen of muliebrity was no less magnificent than when she held my gaze at first, sitting before that wooden altar to servitude. Her countenance, characterized by a grave and dignified beauty, free from any transient expression, effused a palpable glow; and her hair, of fine texture, seemed to trap within its fibers the golden hue of the sun. Her eyes were clear and almond-shaped; her brow wide; her nose and mouth were delicately formed, the top lip protruding slightly, providing her an adorable *moue*. I could continue describing her to the most minuscule of details, but I trust that I have given the reader enough of a picture of this woman for his mental satisfaction.

Holding her chin, I raised her head until she met my gaze.

"I do not bite," said I, trying to add some levity to the moment, because I knew that what Virginia felt was nothing but sadness and despair. I wanted to communicate to her a thorough reassurance that she looked briefly at a master for the last time. But how could I, when my consequent course of action was unclear even to me?

"My name is Stanton Roget. What is your family name, Virginia?"

She looked down again. "I have none, sir," she whispered. I made her look at me for the second time.

"Let us make something clear," said I. "There is no need to address me as 'sir'. Mr. Roget is fine, or if you are so inclined, simply as Stanton. Do you understand?"

I noticed her eyes slightly widen at my snubbing of convention. She nodded reluctantly.

"Yes—sir," she said.

"What?" I mocked.

"Yes—" she struggled and fell silent. Her bare feet now came to my attention.

"Do you have shoes?" I asked, and she denied she did. "Come, let us find you some shoes."

I remembered passing a shoemaker on my morning walk, and to him we proceeded, I with the satchel and Virginia following close behind. I wished that I had had eyes on the back of my head in order to see what types of expressions came over Virginia's face, whether incredulity or pity at her new master's apparent loss of his mental faculties.

A client in stockinged feet sat inside the cobbler's shop, waiting. Seeing no clerk, I rang the bell on the counter until an elderly man in a black apron came out, holding a pair of shoes. He handed them to the man waiting, who proceeded to try them.

"Can I help you, sir?" he asked, glancing behind me at Virginia.

"Do you have any ready-made shoes that may perhaps fit her?"

"Her?" he asked in surprise.

"Yes—her," said I, darkening my tone somewhat in case he had planned a retort.

He removed a tape measure from around his neck and knelt on the floor to measure one of Virginia's feet. At first she pulled her foot back, but then, at my urging, replaced it until the shoemaker completed his task. The other customer, I noticed, had forgotten about his shoes and stared at us. The shoemaker went to a room behind the counter and returned with a cumbersome pair of ladies' boots. Though I do not purport to know a woman's affinities, I immediately rejected them and asked for a more delicate pair. He returned shortly with a more appealing set.

"Will these fit her?" I asked him.

"They should," he said.

Upon the counter lay an illustrated catalog of shoes. I turned to the women's shoe section, brought Virginia closer, and directed her to look through it until she found a pair exactly to her liking. Apprehensively she began her search while I completed the purchase. I directed the shoemaker to make the same shoes that Virginia had chosen from the catalog, and of the finest materials available. After filling out the order, we left the shop, I with her new shoes slung by tied laces about my shoulder. I did not wish Virginia to wear the shoes yet, until she had bathed her dirt-caked feet.

At the hotel, I told the proprietor that I desired a warm bath prepared in my room. Then I inquired about another room for Virginia. He answered, regretfully, that no more were vacant. After some thought, I asked for a cot, which request, though obliged, was met by the most astonished of expressions. Indeed, under normal circumstances, I would not have considered remaining in the same sleeping room with a woman not my wife. But the unsual circumstances relaxed my scruples somewhat.

I bade Virginia to sit while I waited for the chamberlains to come and fill the bath. When they came, and were done, and the water was steamy, I poured in it the fragrant soaps. Then I called Virginia into the toilet. There was no doubt in my mind that her impression was that she was to bathe me, no matter how ridiculous, to my own ears, that sounded.

"The bath is ready for you, Virginia."

"For me?" she asked, incredulous.

"There are clean towels there. I will be in the next room."

I brought her satchel into the toilet and left her to her bath. At that moment a chamberlain arrived with a cot. I went out briefly to purchase a paper to find out any more news about the conflict. I was concerned to be caught in enemy territory if the situation worsened; we were no longer one nation, but a fractured Israel, and instead of in Dan I found myself in Beersheba, among the Baals.

Returning to the room, Virginia was still at her bath. Presently, the splashing of water ceased. When she appeared dressed in a cerulean dress with white hem about the calves, and with the shoes I had purchased for her, I was in the process of opening the cot and testing its sturdiness. She stood with her satchel grasped in both hands before her.

"Lay it down," said I, to which she did; and "Sit down," to which she did also. I sat on the cot.

"Tell me, Virginia, what did you expect when I purchased you?"

"I thought—to serve in your house."

Though soft spoken, her tone was even, and I was surprised at the quality of her diction. Her speech, in a clear but not pronounced Southern accent, was well spoken and devoid of solecisms, denoting an education not usually found among those in her position.

"You appear educated. Can you read?"

"Yes, sir."

"And write?"

"Yes."

"How unusual" I remarked. "I mean—for slaves an education of your level is not common."

"I was born into a kindly family, sir. My mother served in the house.

The master was very fond of me and had the governess instruct me along with his own children."

"You were quite fortunate."

"Yes, very much so. However, after he died I was sold."

"With your mother?"

"She was sold also, but to another family. I learned she died soon afterward."

"I'm sorry to hear that."

"Thank you, sir."

"And your next owner: was he a good man also?"

I noticed a hesitation, but then: "Yes, sir."

"Sir! Now what did I instruct you?"

"Yes—Mr. Roget."

"That's better. I take it you served in the house?"

"Yes."

"Let me tell you of myself now," said I. "As you can probably guess, I am not a Southerner. I have just inherited a plantation not far from here. My father recently passed—"

"Plantation?" she asked.

"Yes. I have not yet decided what course of action to take regarding this dubious boon that has come my way. I am a widower with two children, and have a home and business in New York. It is not my intention to permanently remain here. Seeing that I have no interest in owning slaves, it is my intention to give you your freedom. I would not like to free you here, for I hear that a freed slave in the South is no different than when a slave; so, if you will accompany me North, I will give you your freedom there. There you can go your way to live your life as you please, or you can remain as my salaried employee to care for my house and children. Currently, I have a housekeeper who has served me faithfully for many years and who I wish to retire, that he may spend his last years in tranquility. You do not have to give me an answer now, but I wish you would give some thought to my proposition."

Virginia sat silent when I finished speaking. Then, in a flash, she wept with joy.

"O, you're a good man—a good man! " she cried. I wanted to answer that there was no one good but God, but it gave me such pleasure to see her happy that I did not want to affect her illusion. She composed herself and seemed embarrassed.

"It is all right," said I, and repeated my assurance until she smiled again.

FIVE

THE SLAVES MEET THEIR NEW MASTER

Riding to the plantation, I advised Virginia to feign a submissive role and to treat me as she would a traditional master until I should direct her otherwise. I wanted to be to the uncircumcised as uncircumcised, not wanting to cause offense.

We were met by the same youthful entourage as before, and then by Mrs. Roget with her maid holding a parasol over her. I introduced Virginia, and Mrs. Roget looked at me with a curious expression, but she nevertheless received me graciously. We sat again in the parlor, and, after bringing me some lemonade, the old negress took Virginia away to expose her, I surmised to what she thought was the girl's new home and domestic duties.

"I see you are putting the money to use," said Mrs. Roget.

"Yes," said I.

"May I ask you how much she cost?"

When I told her the quite steep amount, the mistress drew in a sharp breath of surprise.

"I have no need for her."

"I don't intend to leave her here."

"I see," she said, looking down at her hands. "I suppose you are better rested today."

"Yes, I am feeling rather well. I wish to see the rest of the estate today."

As before, one of the slave children was sent to find the mulatto overseer. I flexed my fingers to prepare myself for the powerful grip of the man when he appeared; he did not disappoint me in our handshake. Outside waited two horses held for us by the oldest slave boy, the same one who calmed the carriage horses at my first arrival. He stood between the two fine beasts with the reigns in his hand and a smile on his face. His name was Jubo. Mrs. Roget asked Antoine to return me in time for dinner. So off we rode, I a bit unsteady on the animal, from the awkwardness with things natural a city life engenders.

The shape of the land was roughly trapezoidal, with a stream passing through it on its western end. The greater part was taken up by cane fields, cut by narrow trails for access, and small plots belonging to the slaves where they grew their vegetables. Beside the main house stood the mill where the cane was crushed and ground; a barn-like structure wherein the ground cane was packaged for shipping to a refinery; another building, the boiling house, deserted, containing three great furnaces, which was no longer operable and had fallen into ruin; and about a half mile from the house a cluster of small cabins, around a larger one, by the vegetable plots, where the slaves lived. We entered one of the cabins to find a pregnant negress lying on a cot. She was asleep, but startled awake at our abrupt entrance. This woman's name was Mary, and she seemed to me so large as to be ready to give birth at any moment. I regretted that we awoke her from her needed rest, but I said nothing while in her presence. But outside, I questioned Antoine about the probability that she might begin to give birth alone (there were no other slaves in the cabins at that time) and he responded quite bluntly that she needed no help with bearing children, and could do it quite as well alone as any animal.

We rode out into the fields and Antoine directed one of the slaves to call the others. Lifting his hands to his mouth, this man gave out such a piercing yell that I would not have been surprised if every slave in the parish appeared. Eventually, from all directions assembled several dozen slaves, men and women, some with machetes tied to ropes about their waists. They stood in a line, their black faces, necks, and, in the men, torsos, gleaming with perspiration. All, despite their age, were stout, with strong arms from the constant cutting in which they engaged.

"This is the new master, Monsieur Stanton Roget," Antoine said aloud, tall astride his horse, and then proceeded to introduce me to the slaves, naming each by name. Each responded with a "Good to see yah, sah," or, "Welcome, sah."

"How are you all?" I asked. One of them wiped the sweat from his brow and replied with a mocking tinge, "Jes fine, sah." At this, Antoine galloped toward him, causing him to jump back, reared in front of him, and then came back to my side. I was slightly alarmed. This slave was named Sam and happened to be the husband of the pregnant woman we had seen in the cabin. The overseer dispelled the slaves and each disappeared among the tall canes to continue their duties.

"I apologize, *monsieur*. They forget their place at times," he said.

"That is all right."

"I always keep them in line."

Indeed, I thought. Never had I seen a sterner negro among his people. But perhaps, by virtue of his light color, he gained the preeminence among them.

As we trod through the fields, Antoine explained to me the process whereby the plant cane was converted into sugar, and the role of the plantation in the process. There was a time when the cane was boiled and refined on the premises, but as skilled firemen became scarce, it grew necessary to send the cane downriver to a larger refinery, where not only sugar was obtained, but by-products such as molasses, rum, alcohol, and even wall-board.

I found the overseer quite cordial, but his manner seemed to me a bit haughty. That was my impression when I first saw him at the house, even before he spoke a word to me. Perhaps he resented the fact that after serving my father faithfully for many years, he was not elevated to a higher position at father's death, although I could not imagine what that position would be, save to become a master himself.

It was nearing sunset, and the expanse of sky behind the house was a fiery orange. Antoine rode with me to the stable where he left me to go to his own house, situated between the main house and the cabins, where he lived alone. Jubo, chewing a piece of cane, was at the stable, and he tended my horse for me. I asked him if he was hungry, and he replied, "Yes, sah. A'm truly hungry." As to what awaited him at the slave cabins, he responded, "Yams, sah, an' carrit soup." As he ran from me, I asked who his mother was and he responded that Agnes was his mother. This was the woman whose husband was sold for stealing several years ago, according to Antoine. But whence the smiles? I asked myself. Was it all a veneer, and did a glimmer of a slave's restless soul shine through at the uncomfortable instance with Sam in the field? It was no marvel that at times slaves would rise up and massacre their masters in their beds. I became horrified when I read of such events, my sympathies going completely to the unfortunate owners. But perhaps many of them deserved some punishment for their inhumanities. It seemed to me that should such an uprising occur on my new plantation, I would at least have time to escape, seeing that the slaves would first concentrate on annihilating their overseer before trying to destroy me. Regardless, I now had a certain anxiety and rather wished I had already decided what to do with my interesting inheritance.

The conversation in the dining-room of the house ended when I appeared at the door. I saw already that the old negress had put my Virginia to work, for, in an apron, she was setting the table. At one end of it sat Mrs. Roget and to the sides her children. The chair at the head of the table, presumably for me, sat empty.

The negress, whose name was Deodra, brought me to the table. Mrs. Roget and the children stood.

"This is Mr. Stanton Roget," she introduced me, "the son of your late father. Mr. Roget, this is my son Thomas, and my daughter Marguerite."

"Pleased to meet you," said Marguerite, who looked much like her mother save that her hair was darker and tied into two pony-tails grafted to the back of her head. She bent down to take up a small box which was by her seat, and presented it to me. I opened it to find a fine meerschaum. Though I did not smoke, I thanked her graciously. The boy had nothing special to distinguish him, save that he spoke loudly and shrilly (his was the voice that was so quickly silenced when I walked in); he liked to bother his sister, for throughout the dinner, Marguerite complained of being kicked under the table.

Marguerite, reminding me of an older version of Andrea, was of the quiet sort, and I noticed that every time Virginia came into the room to serve a dish or to take one away, she would look at her and follow her with her eyes so raptly that I thought she, perhaps because of Virginia's beauty, was rather fond of and fascinated by her.

Deodra, it seemed, was quite content to have an assistant, for I only saw her perhaps once or twice during the meal. Virginia rarely looked at me as she carried out her duties quietly, sitting on a small stool in a corner of the room ready to perform a task if instructed. I found my eyes frequently wandering to her position, where they remained for some time until someone at the table addressed me and I turned to reply. I found myself continuing to admire Virginia's beauty as she sat resting her hands in the concave fold of her apron on her lap. I was fascinated by her profound detachment from what was occurring around her. She seemed to be able to concentrate her attention on something commonplace, and be far away, yet present immediately if she was needed. I imagined such was a mechanism of the mind all slaves performed to keep their sanity: a temporary, albeit only mental, escape from their awful reality. She seemed a perfect disciple of Epicurus, who taught that in one's mental life, one should contemplate pleasures rather than pains; physical pain can be endured by the habit of thinking of happy things in spite of it.

Tapping my wine glass with my fork, I beckoned for Virginia to come fill it. She stood by me and poured wine from a bottle. When my glass was half filled, I touched her hand, indicating her to stop. At that moment she looked at me and I at her. A smile I gave her, and she let one creep ever so slightly across her lips. Mrs. Roget demanded that her glass be filled also, in a tone of voice that I knew she had been using on Virginia all the while I was touring the grounds. When Virginia filled her glass, without thanks she was sent to sit on her stool.

"How has Virginia been performing?" I asked Mrs. Roget.

"I think she needs more experience, but Deodra will instruct her," she said.

"Truly?" asked I. "Rather, I think that she has been performing quite wonderfully."

With the compliment I raised my glass to Virginia. Another small smile passed by her lips, and then she lowered her eyes. Marguerite looked at me and smiled satisfactorily. Mrs. Roget drank her wine, staring darkly at me over her glass.

The thud of heavy boots caused me to turn to the door. Antoine Chevaux, hat in hand, bowed slightly toward Mrs. Roget.

"What is it, Antoine?" Mrs. Roget asked.

"The mill will not be ready for our cane until the day after to-morrow," he said, addressing himself partly to me.

"Very well, Antoine, just get us the best price." Mrs. Roget said.

Mr. Chevaux bowed again, but before straightening noticed Virginia for the first time. His glance lingered on her for a moment, like that of a painter who catches sight of a beautiful scene and forgets about aught else, committing the vision to memory to later be elaborated on canvas. Virginia raised her eyes, meeting his but for a brief moment before Chevaux turned and departed.

Supper being ended, and the children sent to their rooms, I was left alone with Mrs. Roget.

"Have you decided what you are going to do?" she asked.

"Yes—somewhat" I replied, "I shall travel back to New York in a week or so to see to some matters there. Then I will return. I will take Virginia with me."

"You will free her?"

"Yes, of course."

"What have you decided regarding the plantation?"

"I do not yet know."

"You must decide."

"I shall."

"There was no need for Alistair to leave it to you. I am quite capable of continuing the business."

"I have no doubt of that."

"Remember, this is *my* home, and Alistair was *my* husb—"

She stopped herself, becoming aware of her inappropriate excitement. "I'm sorry," said she, with lowered eyes.

"Well—thank you for a fine supper, Mrs. Roget," said I, "Virginia and I shall be back to-morrow."

"When will you return from New York?"

"Perhaps after two or three weeks."

"But you will return?"

"Yes."

"Can you not return sooner?"

"I have my children to attend to."

"Oh, I see—but you will return?"

"I said within two or three weeks," I repeated, concerned about her anxiety. "Is anything the matter?"

"No, there is nothing."

Virginia had a final duty of clearing the table and washing the dishes. I went out to the stable and drove back to the house a cart for our transport back to the city. The land was dark, and a bluish haze covered the fields. A host of nocturnal creatures made me to know their presence, and a dog barked in the distance. I sat and waited for Virginia, wondering whether Mrs. Roget wanted me there or not. She confused me with her changes in mood. Perhaps she feared to be left alone because of the slaves; thoughts of blood spattered sheets came into my mind without invitation.

In time, Virginia ran out of the house to where I was, and mounted to sit beside me, I extending my hand to aid her. She dropped by me with a relieved sigh.

"How was it?" I asked.

"I think the mistress does not like me very much," she said.

"No matter; you will see her no more after a week."

I alerted the horse and we pulled out. The moon was in its old gibbous phase, a white crescent floating in the heavens. We rode through the pale light with our luminous destination in the distance, like a New Jerusalem already descended and waiting for us to enter its pearly gates.

By and by, I felt Virginia lean against my shoulder, and glancing at her, found her asleep. In that position we entered the city and she did not wake until I stopped before the hotel. She followed me sleepily to the room, the eyes of the proprietor at the desk following us up the staircase. In the room, I fought all of Virginia's declarations that she should sleep on the cot and I on the bed, until I physically claimed my territory by bounding on the cot. This act of mine caused her so much laughter, that she finally accepted my self-sacrificing courtesy and nestled into the soft and comfortable bed.

From my vantage, and amid frequent turnings through the night as I strove to find an acceptable position on my meager bedding, I glanced at her sleeping form, illuminated by a sliver of light from outside. Slumber seems to me a merciful agent, for it brings peace even to those who during the day are objects of suffering. In the night, in sleep, the tears are blotted and the cries stifled. I tried to imagine what a torture Virginia found in her position, one with a sensibility, culture and knowledge far above the simple minds of her peers. Ignorance is bliss, as they say, and a simple mind will long persist in simple things. But when that mind can read and comprehend literature, how an affliction it must be not to be able to run free among the hills, or to have to answer to any man who says you are *his*, as a dog or a horse.

SIX

TRAPPED IN THE SOUTH

The proprietor of the hotel seemed relieved at our departure. For the next week we lived at the house while I became more acquainted with the life of a planter. From financial records, I found my father to have been quite an astute business man, making a large profit practically every year, wisely adding new slaves and augmenting his fields in times of growth, and reducing operations in times of loss. I could now see why he could trust the business to no one but a careful manager skilled in the workings of labor and finance. Wanting to maintain the riches in the family, or at least one part of it, he chose me. I realized that if I remained and continued the enterprise, I could be fabulously wealthy. Indeed, I seemed to be so already; but like flowers, mammon must be nourished and tended in order to grow— but I did not care to linger around this particular patch.

During this time, I became better acquainted with the slaves, one night visiting their large, common cabin while they were eating. They were very startled at my presence, so much so that those seated eating at the rough wood table stood abruptly, knocking over their cups and plates. Apparently, my late father hardly visited the slave cabins; and when he did, it was with some retributive object in mind.

After reassuring them of my purely social visit, and bringing them to my side, so to speak, they bade me to sit at the head of their table, a slave named Cotter, the elder among them, giving me his seat. Agnes, Jubo's mother, served me a watery stew of vegetables with a few bones for flavor, and cut for me a generous slice of cornbread. Despite the humility of the fare, I found it all quite good, and enjoyed my visit, questioning them and learning from them.

Once in their confidence, the slaves complained to me of Antoine Chevaux as being always a stern taskmaster who was wont to ride upon them and kick them with his foot. I promised to look into the matter. In this they rejoiced, and even more when I announced a proposition that I had not yet mentioned to Mrs. Roget, but planned to. From that point onward, the slaves were to be paid wages for their labor. This was met by an almost hyperbolic surprise, in the manner of negroes, accompanied by a myriad of exuberant "Thank you, sahs".

Mrs. Roget understandably objected to my plan, telling me that in the South, it was simply not the way things were done. I countered by quipping that a master such as I was the inevitable product of a marriage between capitalism and feudalism. During that week, I further incensed the mistress by bringing the pregnant Mary into the house because I discovered that she was overdue by some time. A doctor was brought to the house, who determined that if Mary did not give birth during the next week, he would return and induce the labor. I allowed her husband Sam to work only for half of the day, and to be with his wife the rest, as well as sleep in the room with her until she gave birth. At one point, I went to see how she was faring and touched her brow to feel for a fever. She took my hand in hers and kissed it, calling me a fine master. But I had quit being a master. It was not my lot or desire to be one. Bonded employment, in the long run, made no economic sense; it was not as profitable, not only because of the expense of feeding and clothing the laborers, but also because the laborers have no opportunity to augment the market with their own capital and experience.

By the end of the week, I was anxious to depart the South. The war continued on its unfortunate way, and regiments were being raised in both sections. In the city, I witnessed a parade whose intent was to attract recruits. An orator waxed eloquent about the need and duty of every individual to protect the homeland because the dam' Yankee wanted to swoop down the Mississippi to deprive him of his liberty and livelihood. He reminded his audience that no longer were they part of the United States, but were now a separate nation with the numbers and the states to prove it. "The Confed'racy" rolled off his tongue as some sacred nomen, to be embraced, worshipped, and to be killed over if necessary. That very day, a multitude of men, young and old, lined up to fight.

Seeing that everything was in order, and having instructed Mrs. Roget on various matters to be accomplished the next month before my planned return, I left one early morning with Virginia. We rode into the city and from there boarded a steamboat. Not wanting to attract undue attention, I again instructed Virginia to feign servitude. She therefore, on the journey, sat at my feet as was the custom of other slaves that we saw, although most of the female ones were in the service of mistresses. I was the only man waited on by such.

After a day on the water, we arrived at Vicksburg, where the ship docked for a long time. When our scheduled time of departure was past by several hours, I went about the ship in search of the steward to inquire about the situation. But he was nowhere to be found. After another while, the captain appeared on the deck with several soldiers to announce the news that all north-going traffic was being arrested at Vicksburg and that the ship was not allowed to travel any further. He was to turn the ship around and travel back to New Orleans, so that some of the passengers, denied their destinations, would at least be able to return to their homes.

There were several northerners on board, two of whom I became acquainted with, and they were understandably chagrined at these developments. The Mississippi was the principal artery connecting the two sections, and without its use, transportation out of the deep South was sorely limited. The meager rail tracks found in the South were mostly in the northernmost states.

As the ship turned around, I met for dinner with my two friends. One was a farmer from Illinois who was visiting family in Mississippi. The other was a student at Oberlin college whose home was in Alabama. The farmer was large and tough, and his attempt at some finer clothing for the journey seemed misguided because they were tight and ill-fitting about his frame, the collar of his shirt so inadequate for his neck that a tie would have been an impossibility.

"Here I wuz ready t' go an' head back home, too. By jimminy, I tol' my sister that if I d'in't go soon, I would'a been caught in this here war'ing mess. I tell her, 'Look-e there how li'l Gordy's runnin' up like they going t' give 'im some gold or somethin' like that.' I tell 'im that th' hull thing's a sham from the gov'nment an' that th' army's hell. I ain't never been in any army but I hear it ain't no fun with all that marchin' an' shootin'. I tell 'im, 'Gordy me boy, take yerself t' staying here t' help your po' ol' momma on th' farm.' But no, wide-eyed like a chickin skered he wants t' join the' army 'cause he says he likes all that shootin' they do an' that it's jus' like shootin' 'possums."

"I doubt it's like shootin' 'possums," the student said.

"That's what I tells 'im."

"I'll prob'ly end up joinin' too."

"Yeh, too?"

"Yep."

"Which army?" I asked.

"Why, the Southern one."

"Th' rebel army," the farmer huffed.

"We're not rebels."

"Sho' yeh is. By jiminy, I don' care one way or th' other what an'body does, but it's strong clear t' me that yeh and yer hull contry is rebels."

"We're not rebels, I said."

"Listen, now, what's this here contry call'd? Ain't it th' United States of America? Now, if states ain't united then they is sep'rate, right? We still the United States, but what are yeh? Yeh is now calling yehselves th' Confed'ret States, right? Now, if we still th' same and yeh changed yer colors, then yeh must be rebels. There ain't no mistakin' it, no sir. What yeh think?"

He asked me this question. I was of the sentiment of the farmer, but at the same time, I did not want to offend the student, and so answered noncommittally, "It is an unfortunate situation."

"You joinin' the army?" the student asked the farmer.

"Me?—what, yeh crazy?" he said.

"If you're not joinin' or nothin', why're you jawing as if you had some stake in the sit'ation?"

"I calls it as I sees it—is all."

"Well, if you don't got some stake in the sit'ation, then jus' keep your trap shut."

"Boy, don't tell me t—"

The air was becoming heated and so I interjected a question to both. "What are you going to do now?"

"Huh?" the farmer asked.

"Now that it seems we will not be able to travel the Mississippi to our destinations."

"I guess we're stuck," said the student.

"Is there no other way?" I asked, hoping that a native such as he would know.

"The other way's the train, but if they're stoppin' the Miss'ippi, then they're sure stoppin' trains too."

"Yeh means we stuck?" the farmer asked, alarmed, as if the fateful revelation finally came to him.

"You said it," returned the student.

I immediately thought of my children and grew worried. I had to find a way to return home. What a terrible misfortune I had fallen into. If only I was able to receive word of them by letter, or else they receive word from me, but I knew that mail service would also become disrupted. There was no alternative, for the moment, but to return to the plantation.

My companions were still sore at each other when I left them for the forward deck. There I found Virginia standing alone, looking out into the wide river and the darkness. The wind flapped her dress about her. I stood by her.

"We will have to return to New Orleans," I said. She looked at me, then down at the shimmering water. "I don't know for how long. There must be another avenue of return, certainly. I will investigate the moment we land."

"I cannot go with you," she said; her tone was faint and desolate.

"Why—I have no intention of leaving you."

"I will only be a burden to you. Alone, perhaps, you will find a way home."

"I promised you your freedom, Virginia."

"I thank you; but I am free already. You must think only of yourself now." She let out a quick sigh. "I'm sorry, sir—my forwardness must offend you. It is my weakness—to become too familiar. I forget my place."

"What is your place?"

"To serve you: and I shall do so faithfully in New Orleans; to continue serving the mistress after you are gone; and to wait patiently for your return, whenever that may be."

I marveled at her words. My one act of kindness seemed to engender in her an eternal devotion. But instead of feeling flattered, I felt perverse. That the catalyst for such loyalty began with an unnatural economic transaction seemed an injustice for both parties, and for the nature of friendship itself.

What had I done when I purchased Virginia? Was she, like Pandora, fated to bring ruin? Not immediately that night, but slowly, slowly she lifted the lid, and though through common sense I resisted the tide that came forth, my strong heart began to prevail over my weak mind. The feeling inside me was foreign, dulled, unused, but springing to life. The greater part of it was led into captivity, buried in a plot under an alabaster stone. But a remnant of it remained patiently waiting for some dew to moisten it and cause it to quicken. It was not altruism that caused me to purchase Virginia; it was not benevolence or pity. It was a sort of affection, the moment my visionary organs fell upon her, small and alone, like a lost lamb.

I greatly feared, and resisted to my utmost, this new development.

Mrs. Roget was surprised when Virginia and I appeared at the house again, as well as somewhat relieved, although she tried to conceal that. My efforts of finding a passage north by boat or train ended in futility; save for walking, the rapid development of the conflict cut off all other access. How long I would remain in New Orleans I did not know, but I strove to make the best of it.

For the next several months, I ran the business while Virginia served at the house. I was glad to see that Mrs. Roget's attitude toward her had softened, and so her work was not made unpleasant. I would often sit on the porch, perhaps composing a letter to Frederick, and watch Virginia play with Marguerite and the slave children. How like a child herself she seemed, an innocent child, running through the grass in her simple dress, laughing in merriment. Marguerite grew closer and closer to her, so that she even attempted to style her hair as Virginia's, and held her hand whenever she was by her. Concerning Frederick, or my children, I knew nothing, for as expected, no mail from them ever came. Nevertheless I sent out letters every week.

The Scriptures wisely admonish men not to give their strength over to women. But how easy to read the wisdom of the ancients and yet treat it like ancient wisdom! Over time my affection for Virginia became so strong that I became slightly irritable if I did not see her. But she knew how to soothe me by bringing to me a glass of wine or lemonade, and sitting by me as I drank it, allowing me to contemplate her. Perhaps what made me morose was that I believed that it was becoming clear to her what I felt, especially when retiring to her room at night she found upon her bed a new dress, a box of candy, or a fragrant nosegay I had gathered myself. To determine the propriety of the gifts, I used Marguerite as a spy, sending her to find out for me what were Virginia's favorite colors or blossoms. But in the morning she failed to give me any indication of her appreciation. This caused me great sadness, and I consoled myself by taking long rides around the estate and remembering when I first saw her, when my unrequited love was not evident. Then I was happier.

In such a sullen mood I one day received Mr. Comstock, the distinguished owner of another plantation about three miles from mine. He came dressed all in white, in an elegant carriage with a negro attendant. I invited him to sit with me in the parlor. There he removed his large hat, gave it to his attendant, and passed a hand over his abundant white whiskers.

"Mr. Roget," he said. "I knew your father well, and we often sat conversing in this very room."

"You are welcome any time, Mr. Comstock," said I.

"Thank you. You appear as gracious as your late father, may he rest in peace. But there is something that has been bothering me."

"What is that?"

"It has come to my attention that you are *paying* your slaves. Is that right?"

"Yes, sir, that is correct."

"You are paying them with money?"

"Yes, sir."

"Now, son, whatever gave you the idea to do that?"

"I thought it would be best. Where I come from, we pay our laborers."

"But where you are *now*, slaves are not recompensed for their work—

at least not in that manner."

"Why not?'

"That is not the way it is done"

"Why not?"

"I did not come here to argue with you, Mr. Roget. What you are doing is not sound."

"Mr. Comstock, what I do on my property—and with my property—is my business."

"Rightly so; but when you do something that upsets the natural order of our society it affects me. Are you aware that rumors of what you are doing are spreading to many plantations in this area?"

"I was not aware of that."

"Soon, you're going to have slaves asking for pay and refusing to work, as happened to me with two slaves of my own already. That situation was swiftly remedied, but I fear that the same confusion and discontent could spread to other areas. That would be extremely dangerous."

"Like I said, Mr. Comstock, what I do here is my business. If your slaves demand to be paid, perhaps you should listen."

"Nonsense! I've never heard such nonsense! You are a disgrace to the legacy of your father."

"Perhaps so," I said; "but my father was a disgrace to me."

The gentleman, disgusted, arose to go. I stood on the porch to watch him depart. As his carriage left, he stuck his head out of the window and shouted, "You shall hear from me again!" At that moment, I gave the threat no thought; but I had no doubt that later, it was he who had a hand in causing me great misfortune.

SEVEN

MY FATE IS SEALED

I n the morning I wrote my weekly letter to Frederick in the usual hope
that it would reach him. As yet I despaired that no letter from him had
reached me, and so I knew nothing of the condition of my girls, though I
was certain that under his care they must have been well.

Mrs. Roget had gone into the city and through the house I walked in
search of Virginia. For the third night that week, I awoke in an almost feverish
state, with my brow wet, and with my mind filled with amorous thoughts.
When asleep, of my dreams, Virginia was the content; and once awake, her
continuance among my clouded thoughts prevented me from resuming
slumber.

Deodra was in the kitchen preparing a meal and did not know
Virginia's whereabouts. I rode my horse out to the slave cabins, and there I
found a little slave-girl named Larena busy in play with a doll made out of a

corn-cob and rags. She informed me that Gina, as she called her, had gone out to the stream. To that place I then rode, seeing Virginia from afar, sitting under a tree in a comfortable copse where the stream widened after a fall to form a small linn surrounded with large stones. Stealthily I approached her and hid behind a tree, like Actaeon, to espy this golden Artemis, though unlike him, safe that she had no power to transform me into prey for my own dogs.

She sat upon a rock, her custom-made shoes next to her, her dress doubled on her lap, her feet dipped in the water. A book was in her hands, and she was hunched over it in rapt concentration.

I took a hard nut from under my shoe and cast it over her into the water. She at once looked up and around; seeing no one, she resumed her reading. I did the same, but with a stone; the poor girl looked up into the boughs over the pond thinking the disturbance was coming from there. I chuckled at my games as I approached her. She turned around at the crunch of twigs under my heels.

"Was that you?" she asked.

"You mean those objects falling into the water?" I asked. "Yes, it was I."

I sat next to her on the rock, with my back to the pond. The boulder gave me room to lean back upon my elbows so that I looked up into Virginia's radiant face.

"What are you reading?" I asked. She closed the book to show me its spine. It was a collection of poems by an author I was not familiar with.

"Are they any good?" I asked, referring to the poems. She nodded her head and paged through the book. Finding the desired page, she lay the book beside her flat so that I could read it. The poem, in two stanzas, was as follows:

All hope in life have I since lost,
I sigh for every breath I take,
No longer willing to serve a host
To sweet air got by God's mistake.
I should have been stillborn from my birth,
Aborted and cast into the ground,
Having the worm-filled earth as for my berth,
And an unmarked marker on my mound.
   What use am I to the world or you,
   A wretched man of mildewed tissue?

When I, of earth, to the earth do go,
And never more shall my name be heard,
No longer will my pen bestow
For love of you, a rhyming word.
No more shall the only beauty that I have,
That is, the art produced by mind and pen,
(Not only for my love, but for my heart a salve),
Ever see the light of day again.
   With me will perish lovely thoughts,
   That of your sight and smell and smile were
   wrought.

"It has the form of a Shakespearean sonnet," Virginia observed.

"Indeed—but poor fellow!" I remarked. "What could be the matter with him?"

"I fancy he is in love," said Virginia, closing the book.

"Have you?"

"Have I?"

"Yes—been in love?"

"No, not I."

I could not believe that. "Never?"

"No."

"Not even once?"

"Never."

"But you have certainly caught the eye of many men."

"Perhaps."

"It would be an absurdity to believe otherwise."

"Why do you say so?"

"You're so beautiful, Virginia," I finally admitted out loud, and it felt like a great burden was lifted from me. She looked away into the slowly rippling water. I took her hand in mine and caressed it, placing her palm against the side of my face; closing my eyes, for a moment, it was the hand of Madeline that I felt. It was summer long past, and the blue Hudson, mealy with a million platinum twinkles, rolled lazily with steaming barges on its back. The water clapped against the rocks and washed them with a pure, refreshing sound. We sat on the bank, mesmerized in courtship, our eyes closed and our minds a factory of dreams. That was long ago, but the mind retains its photographs diligently, as if those illusory images were etched forever in that sentient matter.

Virginia withdrew her hand and stood quickly, the book dropping into the water. She ran to a tree and stood with one hand against it. I went to her and found her weeping. I turned her to me gently and beheld her delicate eyes filled with tears. Had I not been stronger at that moment, the sight of such a frail, gentle creature weeping such, would have moved me also to tears. But I held her, trying to comprehend what was the reason for her sadness.

"Why won't you allow me to love you?" I asked. "Are you afraid of me? Have I done any harm to you? Tell me now, and I shall repent."

"You have done me no wrong," she said.

"Then why do you spurn me? Why do you weep?"

"Don't—" she beseeched me.

"I must know!"

She swallowed hard, and wiping the tears said: "You cannot love me."

"Why," I asked, my heart breaking. "Why so?"

Her moistened eyes were so large and luminous, that I beheld myself in them as in a looking-glass.

"Deodra, Agnes, Mary, they are black. See how black as soot they are! But look"—I held up her hand before her face—"how a mere breath of color separates you from me. There is no difference. Is this the reason? Oh, do not be silent. Answer me!"

Virginia shook her head sorrowfully and was about to speak when her eyes caught the bounding black form of one of the negro children who came running across the field. As he approached, I could see his excited face, intent on his duty of delivering, no doubt, an important message to his master.

He ran up to me and stopped, his speech arrested by the necessary lungfuls of air he needed to restore his body after his exercise. When finally the lad was able to form words, he informed me that the mayor of the city and several soldiers were waiting for me at the house. The announcement surprised me, and I wondered what was the purpose of their visit. I sent the boy back, and he ran with that effervescent joy of a child delighting in a good deed done. I tried to lead Virginia with me, but she resisted my pull.

"Leave me here, Stanton—please," she said, turning from me. It was the first time she had called me by my Christian name. My horse, I saw, had strayed far, so I fetched it and I rode back to the house, looking back once to see Virginia, standing by the tree so picturesquely that a painter would have rejoiced to capture the scene on canvas.

The mayor of New Orleans stood over an elegant ivory chess set on display in the parlor. Two men sat on the davenport, officers in gray. Deodra, I saw, had served them. When I walked in, the mayor looked up and walked toward me with a hand outstretched.

"Mr. Roget, it is a pleasure to meet with you. I am Mayor John Monroe."

He walked with me, my palm still clasped to his, to the two officers.

"This is Lieutenant-Colonel Samson Oak," the mayor said of one elderly officer who was completely bald but possessed a most magnificent beard, so long it flowed down to his chest, and square-cut so that he looked as if he was carrying a feed sack on his chin. One of his eyes was defective, and the pupil looked askance. The other younger officer was Major Andrew Piecemeal, a tall, rather handsome and elegant-looking fellow.

We all sat down, and I helped myself to a cracker from a tray on the table.

"What can I do for you gentleman?" I inquired guardedly, sensing the visit was not purely convivial.

"You have a fine house, Mr. Roget," the mayor said and the officers agreed with nods. "I am happy to see that nothing has suffered in the transition from your late father to yourself. Your father was a fine and honorable man, who at times donated generously for the benefit of the city."

Deodra came into the room and stood by me. "Do you gentlemen need anything else?" I asked. They were satisfied and so I sent Deodra back.

"Lieutenant-Colonel Oak is over the 17th Louisiana, organized only two weeks ago, and Major Piecemeal is his adjutant," the mayor said.

"Preparations for the war are well under way?" I inquired.

"Yes, thankfully, everything is falling into place. We are here to ask you, Mr. Roget, to command a company. Your late father, honorable man that he was, would have been the first to volunteer. There are still several companies needed to complete the 17th and we are in need of a man of your integrity and intelligence."

"You want me to command a company?"

"Yes, Mr. Roget."

"You understand that I am from New York?"

"Yes, we understand."

"And you want me to be a part of the southern army?"

"Actually," Oak said, "you have no choice."

"What do you mean I have no choice?"

The mayor anticipated the old officer. "What Commander Oak means is that your situation is a bit sensitive at the moment." His cordiality annoyed me; had he been a bit blunter, it would have been more in line with the graveness of the situation, as far as I was concerned. "You see, Mr. Roget, estate owners *are expected* to volunteer their services, particularly in leadership positions, to the cause. It sets a good example to the citizenry."

I tried in vain to indicate the contradiction. "But I am not sympathetic to the South," I said. The officers became visibly disturbed.

"You, Mr. Roget, are a property owner on Southern soil," the mayor said.

"What if I refuse?" I asked.

"If you refuse," the adjutant spoke for the first time, "you will be arrested."

"Arrested?" I asked surprised. "For what?"

"We are in time of war," Oak said. "In such times the rights of men become limited. If you do not comply with our request, an arrest is our only recourse."

"But how can I, in good conscience, serve with the enemy of my section of the country?"

"We understand the difficulty," the mayor said. "But you, by being a northerner, are, for that reason alone, an anomalous element in our midst. In addition to that, may I point out, we have had reports of wholly alien and subversive methods you are employing with your slaves. So we are being rather generous with you. We are giving you the chance to escape imprisonment by serving in the southern army. The compensation is generous, the time of service hopefully short, and you will be doing yourself and your estate a favor."

The ominous final words of Mr. Comstock came to mind. I had no idea that I would create such a storm by what I thought were humane and reasonable acts.

"How long would I remain under arrest?"

"Indefinitely," Piecemeal said.

"As I said before," the older officer said. "In times of war—"

"Yes, I know," I cut him off; "but this is preposterous! A northerner serving in the southern army! An innocent man imprisoned!"

Deodra appeared, hearing my agitated voice. I dismissed her.

"What will you decide, Mr. Roget?" the mayor asked.

"I need some time to think," said I.

"Very well," Piecemeal said. "I will return tonight. But let me warn you, sir, I will arrive with soldiers. You will come with us one way or the other."

I stood on my feet, incredulous at my ill-treatment. I was damned in whatever I decided. I certainly could not allow myself to be arrested. An indefinite incarceration was not appealing to my sense of urgency. My only recourses were either to flee or accept my assignment in the southern army until—and it was only a thought in a moment of understandable despair and uncertainty—I found an opportunity to escape it.

I shook my head at them in disbelief, and they took my action as a sign to end our meeting. We shook hands automatically, and they left me in the mayor's personal carriage.

Deodra, accustomed to waiting upon her masters in moments of distress and potential histrionics, returned, and having heard all and understood all, tried to lead me to sit. But I shook her off, needing no help, and began to pace around the parlor.

EIGHT

A LAST SUPPER

After accomplishing nothing mentally or materially by my pacing, I sent one of my boys to prepare my horse for me. I took a swift gallop on the road into the city and stopped at the offices of my rotund attorneys, whom I had not seen in a long while, but whose help, they affirmed, I could always count on.

A curious little man, whom I took to be the Finlay of McLee, McLee and Finlay, met me. I say curious because I could not at first see him since he was lost behind his large desk in a jungle of books and papers. His head emerged like that of a sleeping cat, suddenly awakened, wide and glassy-eyed, only to squeal "Go into that office there." I did so and found only one McLee, who welcomed me heartily and bade me to sit down.

He listened patiently to my story, and as he did so his face darkened with concern. He then perused through several books which importance I took to matter to my situation. His research done, he flopped back into his sturdy chair and exhaled a generous sigh.

"I am at a loss, Mr. Roget," he said regrettably.

"Can you do nothing at all for me?" I asked.

"There is no precedent for this situation that I can find. I agree with you that it is absolutely preposterous."

He agreed to come to the house in the evening in order to represent me against my military oppressors. I asked if the other McLee could come also, their combined mass to weigh in my favor, but he was away.

When I arrived back at the house, Mrs. Roget, having returned, met me with an astonished look. Deodra, having a full intelligence of the matter, had enlightened her; I had no need to enter into any lengthy explanations with Mrs. Roget. She took me into her parlor, and there we talked until Deodra called us for supper.

The dining room seemed darker, although all the lamps shone with their usual intensity. Deodra went about her service silently, working very carefully and avoiding my eyes. Mrs. Roget also ate quietly, speaking only to calm the children when they became rambunctious. I ate deliberately myself, tasting every sip of wine and every morsel of meat, not knowing when Judas and his throng would arrive.

Every time the kitchen door opened, I looked to it eagerly, hoping my Virginia would appear with the next course in her arms, stately and clean in her cottons, her apricot-colored face imperturbable in its expression, her demeanor insouciant about my presence, a glow of nubile femininity about her whole and enchanting person; but all that appeared was her older and blacker image, Deodra, the features of her weathered face a deterioration of the one which I loved to gaze on.

Where was Virginia? Surely Deodra had informed her compatriot while I was in the city. But she was not here, at least to, by the sight of her pearl-drop eyes, encourage me in their luminance; not that everyone was not concerned—they were. But none of it mattered to me. I did not care if Mrs. Roget had shed tears of blood if Virginia had not an ounce of concern, meretricious or genuine, for me.

Had I not saved her from an ignoble fate when I brought her and took her under my care? Did I not share in the grief of her past and pity her slavehood? I began to grow angry that I had generated feelings for this girl—frail, fragile feelings that are the weakness of even the strongest men. That inner maelstrom of helpless affection is a thing to be reckoned with; it is an entirely selfish vibrancy, for I wished to possess Virginia. I wished her to be in me at times, to see through my eyes and breathe through my nostrils; to feel those things I felt, and to love those things I loved. I grew that way with Madeline after years of matrimony. The process of becoming one flesh is indeed marvelous. It is an act and a process, and the process goes on forever; or until Providence should see it wise to rend that flesh asunder, as was done to me, and the nerves and sinews and veins full of blood we shared were shred, leaving my soul lacerated, as Frederick well knows, for he was there those nights when I filled my pillow with howls and drenched it with my tears. *Unfair, unfair! How could a rat, a dog, a horse have life, and you not at all, my Madeline?* Was there no just balance in heaven where motherhood, sincerity, virtue, kindness, gentleness, patience, meekness, and tenderness was reckoned to one's favor? I came to conclude the lot of all is the same. Rogues live happily while the innocent perish in their innocence. *And, you were innocent, dear Madeline, taking pity on even the smallest of sparrows found sometimes fallen on our yard. On you was my grief well spent. Rightly did I feed the grass on your grave with the dew of my body, shed generously so that every blade should have sustenance.* But sometimes I find it a mockery that a man, who with a bit of bread and water, can march a hundred miles, or at a command, run out in war to face the lethal hordes, may wither, like some useless shrub, from a broken heart. The rib is his Achilles heel, taken from near his heart, and exposing that precious organ to all manner of vicious vicissitudes.

"Children, you may go to your chambers," the voice of Mrs. Roget interrupted the thoughts of my mind. Marguerite and Thomas left their seats to happily bound up the stairs, their plates covered in an admixture of unwanted greens and potatoes. As if Deodra had somehow a spy-glass trained on us, she promptly appeared and whisked everything away that was not involved in Mrs. Roget's and mine individual suppers.

Mrs. Roget looked at me. I met her eyes and for a second received of her a different impression than what was normally my perception. She looked rather attractive. Her blond mane fell like crepe around her shoulders, and her long face, until then usually covered with a gloominess I took to be from the death of her husband, reflected a new dolefulness, perhaps out of solicitude for me.

"When shall they come?" she asked.

"I expect them soon," was my response. "Such perfidious events usually occur after suppers."

"And you shall go with them?"

"I have no choice."

"What will happen to the estate?"

"Mr. Chevaux is a capable man—"

"What will happen to you?"

Mrs. Roget was forced to take up her napkin to blot a tear that had escaped from her eye.

"I expect to return, surely.   From what I've heard, officers have a higher survival rate than their men."

"I wish my husband had never asked you to come here.   Your life has been thrown into turmoil."

"Yes," I responded and thought of my girls back home.   It had been long since I had to answer one of Andrea's childish questions, or looked upon the face of Madeline and seen in it the reflection of her namesake.   There was no use in an absolute dejection.   I would see them again, I had no doubt. Tribulation should never be augmented by a dearth of hope—such I have learned in my life.   And hope, at that moment, to me, was a precious commodity.

"I will be in my room," said I.   "When Mr. McLee arrives, fetch me immediately."

With that I left the table.   Mrs. Roget sat silently, and I felt her eyes follow my departure.

On the way to my chamber, I stopped before Virginia's door.   It was shut.   I put my ear to the door but heard nothing.   She was in there, I knew. My hand touched the knob but did not move it.   I shook my head and moved on to my chamber.   Once inside, an intense weariness overtook me, compounded by the sedative effect of a full stomach.   I fell headlong into my bed, and with my face buried in my pillow, fell fast asleep.

NINE

I JOIN THE REBELS

L ethargy at its most extreme prevented me from executing except the minutest movements of my body in response to a heavy knocking at the door. With great exertion I betook myself to my feet and trudged to the door to open it.

"The Major and Mr. McLee are downstairs. They have just arrived," said Mrs. Roget, wringing her hands in front of her. Behind her stood Deodra. I responded that I would be down shortly, admitted Deodra, and closed the door. Some cool water from the wash basin on my face and neck awoke me fully, while Deodra went about the room packing those articles that I would need in my adventure. Sitting on the bed, I watched her work quietly. Never had I met a negro more silent. It seems the natural propensity of her race to indulge in loquacity, but Deodra was a curious exception. I could not tell her age. She may have been forty, fifty, or sixty years of age. In negroes, verbosity is matched only by an incredible delay in the physical consequences of senility.

"Deodra," I drew her attention. "Is anything wrong with Virginia?"

The negress looked up briefly from her folding of my shirts and responded, "No, Mas'r Roget."

"She is in her room, is she not?"

"Yes, sah."

"Did you not tell her of my departure?" I asked and Deodra said nothing. "Surely, you must have told her. Did she say anything? Did she do anything?"

To my astonishment, Deodra did not answer. "I am speaking to you, Deodra," I emphasized.

I drew close to her. "Why has not Virginia come to me? Did I not buy her out of the goodness of my heart to save her from an ignoble end? Did I not lavish tenderness and kindness on her and provide for all her wants? Did I not give her a home to live in, and the freedom to do as she wishes? Then why does she not come forth? Is her heart so stony that even the most pathetic of affections cannot penetrate it? *Woe is me, for I am undone! Because I am a man of unclean lips!* Deodra, do you know why my lips are unclean? Do you?"—at this I was full in front of the terrified negress, terrified because my voice was raised and my eyes no doubt reflected a sullen indignation; "because I let escape from them the most unconscionable oath ever devised by man. I told her that I loved her. What a fool I was to waste my affections on such a surly, scrawny nigger. And that is all she is, a nigger and a slave. And she is my slave. Bring her here at once! At once, I said!"

I grew more fierce as my speech progressed, and caused the poor Deodra to jump aside and run out of the room. And I truly was fierce. There was a great anger in my heart which felt uncontrollable. I felt betrayed and misused.

Almost immediately, the door opened again and behind it stood the two women, Virginia in a sleeveless cambric nightgown, exposing her thin and fragile arms. Her hair was covered in a kerchief and her juvenile face looked at me with such an exquisite delicateness that it caused me to temporarily lose whatever fury I had and replaced it with a helpless attachment.

I bid Deodra to leave us both. When she did not move, to my astonishment, I rushed forward with my hand upraised. The negress disappeared and left her sire to face me.

"Enter and close the door," I told Virginia and she did so, her head lowered. "Complete packing my belongings."

Virginia passed me without a glance and took up where Deodra had left off. I sat in a large chair. The following I am loath to relate, but I must. I saw for myself to what immoral depths a man will go whose mind is racked with misery, and who is encouraged in a modern Sodom to imitate the practices of his neighbors. What caused me to lose all modesty I could only guess; my lack of restraint was wholly uncharacteristic of my demeanor, and the extent of it shocked me when I was cool enough to ponder what I had essayed.

"Come here," I called to Virginia, "and change my shoes."

Virginia brought the shoes that I had indicated and knelt before me, beginning to untie my laces. I stared at her as she did so—my emotions a mix of pity and marked aggression, of pure affection and hopeless lust.

When she had succeeded in removing my shoes, and was about to put on the new pair, I kicked all of the articles aside, reached out, and pulled Virginia onto me. When she resisted, I took her face with both my hands and pulled her lips unto mine. She broke away with a cry as I kissed her violently, and stood aghast with mouth open.

"Stanton—!" she hissed in fright, but I was up and on her, her fragile arms in my strong grip. "No, please—!" she cried as I tried to devour her lips as food with an insatiable appetite. At last, she was completely in my power, exposed, absolutely mine. And what I was doing was entirely legal in this foreign place in which I found myself. No one could charge anything against me. Virginia was my property and I could do with her what I wished.

Virginia wept so profusely that her words, when she attempted to speak, came out as gibberish. Finally her hot tears and pitiful whimpering arrested me. I heard Andrea and not her.

Taking advantage of the respite, she broke from me and held a fist, a handful of gown in it, protectively under her trembling chin.

At once my energies left me as sap through a bore in a tree, and I collapsed into such a shower of tears that it matched only the collective tearage I had spent on Madeline.

"Virginia!" I cried, "Forgive me! Forgive me! I know not what I do," and I fell to my knees, then humbled myself further to kiss her small feet; but she fled to the door. For a brief moment she looked at me, and I at her. In her face I saw neither anger nor pity, only a deep and relentless sorrow. I shamefully lowered my head into my hands and heard the door open and shut.

Sitting on the floor a long while, I lamented over what I had done. I wanted to find Virginia and make amends, if that was at all possible. I felt a tremendously sharp pain in my heart, as if a knife with a dull and corroded blade was embedded there. The only other time I had felt that pain was after Madeline died. It lingered for a long while afterward, worsening at night when I had to retire to my chamber alone, without companion. I could not bear to think that I had lost her forever, and that never again would I see her except, if true, on the golden streets of Paradise; but even such cherished beliefs were no consolation to present grief. A helpmeet is the greatest gift a man can receive, far surpassing wealth or prestige. Time only forges the relationship, and builds one out of twain. To have that serene, comforting oneness rent asunder is the greatest of all crimes. No more sweet caresses; no more gentle longings; no more morning kisses; no more patient ear or wise tongue; no more considerate and unconditional love. The one who was there with me, who was able to be seen and touched and smelled, whose body was warm, whose mind was acute and evident in sparkling eyes—that one, is no more. She is replaced with memories that satisfy when asleep but starve when awake. To think that at one time there existed one person in this world, a world so large and uncontrollable, that understood me and gave some order to my life, and then one day, for no good reason, was gone, was so absurd that I had to reconvince myself of its reality every day.

And now Virginia was gone also. It was no outside agent that removed her, no act of God, but vile me. After my ignoble act, she seemed lost to me forever. Burdened with emotion, which I sought to conceal, I proceeded downstairs.

I found my attorney, a muffin in one hand and a glass of milk in the other, in vigorous discussion with Major Piecemeal when I entered the parlor. Mrs. Roget, who was sitting near them, stood when I entered. Mr. McLee put down his alimentation and came to me.

"I have been fighting for you, Mr. Roget," he said earnestly; "but I find there is nothing that can be done at the moment. The commander has martial law behind him, and it seems you are forced to comply, unless, of course, you wish instead to be incarcerated. But I advise against this."

"Yes, I know all the details," said I. "I will leave with him."

"Very good," the officer said. "Your baggage has been placed in the carriage awaiting us outside. The military is not a game, sir. If you take it lightly, or attempt to sabotage your position, you will be dealt with most severely,"

"Does it matter that I know next to nothing about the military life?" I asked.

"That does not matter. Most of the officers know as little as the privates. But you will be trained."

"Where will we be going now?"

"To the officer's camp, outside Orleans, near B—"

"I will continue to do everything I can," the attorney encouraged. "Rest assured that McLee, McLee and Finlay will not let you down."

Mrs. Roget came to me, took my right hand in her hands, and said to me, "I will daily pray for your safety and hastened return."

A greater volubility would have defeated the honesty of Mrs. Roget's concern, and her terse exhortation was a better farewell than a thousand good-byes. I kissed her hand, bringing a roseate tinge to her wan complexion, and waved to the children, who I suddenly noticed standing awkwardly on the stairs. Marguerite sprang from the side of her brother and embraced me about the waist, sobbing Mrs. Roget pulled her from me. I followed the adjutant out of the door.

The sight from the veranda would have intoxicated a more ambitious man with feudal power. All of my negroes stood in two columns, facing each other, in front of the house, in direct line with a carriage waiting on the river road at the other end. They held torches and were watched over nervously by several young soldiers in gray. The slaves looked up at me when I appeared, their black, shiny faces coming alive like burnished bronze from the glow of the flames. They were all there, as far as I could see, young and old, weak and stout. There stood Cotter, Agnes, Jubo, Sam and his wife (she holding her little one), others with names like Josiah, Cuba, Kezia, George, Jim, and Sukey, and still others whose names I could not remember. The soldiers that stood vicariously as guards in case some disorder arose were dwarfed in size by most of my negroes, and would have been in jeopardy, despite their weapons, if, upon my order, the slaves attempted to secure my freedom by force. Despite my docility, I felt as secure as Christ in the garden, who knew he could count on legions of angels from his Father. I had my own legion also, being a shade darker, but at that moment no less glorious in character than those from heaven.

"How came my slaves to be here?" I asked the Major.

"They assembled on their own accord, and have been in that position since I arrived. Despite the alleged abuses of your role, your slaves are amazingly well behaved."

Leaving Mrs. Roget, Mr. McLee, and the recently appeared Deodra on the veranda, the Major and I walked through the negro gauntlet. At once the narrow passage became suffused with groanings, prayers, and wishes for a safe return. "Lawd be wid ye," "We's gonna miss ya, Mas'r," and "Perserve him, Lawd," were among the recitations that filled my ears. Antoine Chevaux, in a fine silk vest and white pants, stepped out from the column and bowed, his mouth set in a sort of mischievous smile and with an affectation of manner distinguishable from the humbler folk about him.

"The slaves are in good hands," he said; and as I walked past him he added: "Particularly Miss Virginia."

I was at a loss to respond to his somewhat awkward comment and so continued my fateful march. Halfway to the waiting carriage, the Major stopped and said to me, "It would be to your advantage to take along a slave,

as an attendant. Most officers have one or two." He said it loud enough for all
of the slaves to hear, and as a result all became quiet. Down the line a torch
detached itself from the others, and the strapping Sam presented himself.

"Mas'r, take me wid you," he said.

I objected immediately. "No, Sam, you have a wife and a child to care
for."

"I know's it Mas'r," he said. "But my wife's cap'ble ob takin' kere ob
de li'l one. You'se been a goodly mas'r to us all, 'specially to me, my wife, and
my li'l one. I'll neber forget, as long as I live, that you took my wife into de
house—de Big House no less—and let her hab her chile there in all comfo't.
Dere has neber been a mas'r in de hole world as kindly and as goodly as you,
sah. So let po' Sam go wid you to take kere ob you. I'se always done what I'se
sup'osed to do, but this time I'll go wid you weder you like it or not, sah."

Such a loyalty I never expected. "If you wish, Sam," replied I.

"Yes, sah, wid all my hart. I'se go wid you," Sam said.

And so our party grew to three. We had almost reached the carriage
when, on an impulse, I turned back and looked at the house. The windows of
the top floor were all dark, save for one, and in its frame of light I saw a figure.
My deficient vision prevented me from distinguishing who it was, but I hoped
it was Virginia. I saw then, in my mind, her cherubic face, and her bright eyes
misted with the charms of youthful innocence. A pang of remorse shook my
body when I remembered what I had done, and I wanted to break away from
my companions, run to her, and embrace her. My inner sorrow convulsed my
body, and I, like a heartless ghost, floated toward the carriage. When I would
return again, I could not know. My departure was doubly bitter, the greater
half because of Virginia, who loathed me because of my perfidy. She had trust
in me. She thought me benevolent. Perhaps no one had ever been so kind to

her; but in my passion I broke that trust. She thought that she could be safe with me, unlike under other masters. But I joined their company, doing the same as they. Given time, I descended also to their depravity. Was it the world in which I found myself that turned me into a senseless beast, or was the beast present from the start within me, waiting for the proper moment, for a time alone, when the propriety taught me from my youth would yield to a speeding heart and a blood hot and thick like lead?

I thought I saw the figure in the window reach out for me; but it could have been the shifting shadows of the boughs against the house. I vowed then to return at all costs, and to, if need be, slay myself before Virginia, if by my death she would be appeased, and pity me.

TEN

MY DILEMMA ELUCIDATED

The officers' camp lay near B——, across the Pontchartrain, by a gorgeous grove of wild orange trees, where sparse fruitage gave clear indication that hungry humans lurked about and took good advantage of it. The general camp was situated two miles up hill, and the very night I arrived, several hundred new recruits were added to it, leading to the sudden addition of dozens of camp fires, pin pricks in the distance.

Major Piecemeal left me once we entered the camp, and promised to join me shortly. The squad of soldiers to whom I was entrusted escorted Sam and I to a tent prepared for my arrival. Once there I thought the soldiers would leave me, but instead they encircled the tent to guard me. How an officer was to lead in an army when he himself was an object of suspicion and had to be closely monitored, staggered my mind. Whose idea it was to detain me and by what design they meant to keep me in accord with their regulations were questions that did not grow weary of remaining in my mind the two hours I waited for the Major to return. But Sam, at least, was my companion in my new and strange surroundings, and his familiar presence greatly comforted me.

My tent was rather two wall tents placed end to end for an office and a bedroom. The office contained a simple secretary, a chair, and a settee. The bedroom was more makeshift, and had for a bed a group of gun-boxes covered in a blanket, another settee, and an apple-box for a small table on which sat a tin cup and basin.

A lantern hung from a cord on the top cross beam of my humble office, and Sam and I sat in its yellow light. I stretched myself back on the settee while Sam squatted on the board floor killing whatever insects happened to crawl up through the cracks. Sam was a powerfully built, large negro, black as they come, so dark that there existed the illusion of a bluish hue about his head and shoulders. His large, protruding brow gave him the general impression of obtuseness, as in most negroes; but one could sense, from his eyes, which were always fixed on whatever he was looking at, without the usual lapse in eye contact necessary to shatter the monotony of vision, that he had a great deal of acuity. Such curious attention I found strange, for negroes never look long in a white man's eyes, and usually mark their conversations with nervous glances in every direction.

There have been incidents of tremendous brutality inflicted on white men by slaves, in which atrocious deeds were committed and much blood shed. Such was the case in Haiti shortly after the French Revolution, and then again at the turn of the century, when practically all of the whites on the island were exterminated. And of course, there was the oft-mentioned uprising in Santo Domingo. On our own soil, the slave Nat Turner earned infamy for his unfortunate rebellion. And who was to know what further convulsions would in time shake this land when the slaves properly organize and arm themselves

against their masters, and in a protracted and sanguinary struggle either achieve
their freedom, or their decimation.

With Sam, alone, I felt no fear, despite the docility that was only a film
covering the turbulence below. Sam had sufficient respect of my good-will,
and I had sufficient comfort in his fealty, to imagine anything negative about
him. I wondered instead about the other officers and their slaves. There were
many who treated their slaves with modesty; but surely, there were others, who
hardened by military life, augmented their given lordship with tyranny. Such a
one I did not wish to be, if some time, under the threat of death, I should find
myself at the mercy of one of my slaves and in need of his assistance for my
survival. But Sam was a good and honest man, and his loyalty seemed beyond
question after his willing enlistment with me.

"Sam," I called to him an hour into our stay. "Did my father treat you
well?"

"Well, Mas'r Roget," he said, "gen'relly he was a goodly mas'r who
neber beat any ob us jus' 'cause he feels like it, like my other mas'r, Mas'r
Douglass."

"Where were you a slave before?"

"Up in Virginy, there's where I was. I grew up there on Mas'r
Douglass' plantation where he growed cotton an' tobacco. But Mas'r Douglass
was given much to drink, and he would drink while his wife was off to church
on de Lawd's day. Then he would get might mad wid us po' niggers 'cause he
saw that we wasn't workin'. I would tell 'im, 'But Mas'r Douglass, it's Sunday.
You sed so youself. You sed that we don't got to work on Sundays.' But when
he was tight he neber remembered what he sed on d'other six days. So he'd
holler an' screem at us an' take his whip and set us a-scamping ebery which way
an' makes us go out in de field and start pickin' de cotton. Then he would
come back less drunk an' whip us again 'cause we was workin' on de Lawd's

day."

"That is the most ridiculous story I have ever heard."

"Yes, sah, midy rid'culous. If it warn't for all de whippin', I wood laugh meself. But he was midy wicked wid that whip."

"And how came you to work for my father?"

"Well, Mas'r Douglass had to sell me off 'cause he got into det on account ob all his drinkin'. That was a shame 'cause that lan' was prosp'rous at de fust while I was growin' up. But when de Mas'r lost his chile to de cough, well, that's when he start de drinkin'. The Mas'r wasn't so mean 'fore he lost Maybelline—das his chile—but he turned so aftaward. Guess he loved his chile so much that't broke his hart to see de Lawd take her so young. She was only eight if I 'member right. Darlingest crittur you've eber sen, wid a face like one ob dem angels in hebben. I know'd that white folks are butiful, but li'l Maybelline was de mos' butiful ob all. I still 'member her. She was the kindliest li'l lady who didn't know 'bout black an' white, 'bout de nigger and de buckra. To her eberyone was de same. She was de on'y white folk I eber cried 'bout."

"And then you were sold to my father?"

"Yes, but not d'rectly. Fust I was a-while in Kentuck and then I was taken here for work on de sugah-land 'cause you need big niggers like me to work de sugah. Down here in Orleans, they don't got too many niggers like me. All's they got—well, mos'—is dem yeller one and dey's no good for sugah-work. Dey's to fine and dere bones is too sof', like de white man's."

"You refer to someone like Virginia?"

"Yes, sah, like Miss Virginny. See's how small she is? And den look at my wife, how big and strong *she* is."

"Yes, Virginia is very fragile."

"Yes, sah, I know'd it."

"And so my father was fair?"

"Consi'rably. I never know'd a Mas'r as kindly as you, but he was kindly hisself sometimes."

The flame of the lantern flickered, causing slight variations in the shadows that decorated my quarters. I looked up at it and thought of Virginia with the warmth characteristic of young lovers dreaming of each other under a full moon, and wishing that space and time should be compressed to enable them to be together. I felt young again and a participant in that flush of romance experienced with a first love. For two years my natural desires lay dormant along with its object. Frederick had long tried to bring to my attention a widow who lived here or an available woman who lived there. But his suggestions fell dead at my feet, my mind and heart having set up ramparts to deflect them. What use had I for common food and drink after having tasted the sweetest nectar of all womanhood? I had picked a rose and it had wilted in my hands. I feared to pick another and experience the same loss and unhappiness. But even more, how could I relight the ashen embers of my heart and expect them to burn with equal intensity?

It was my greatest desire to place my arms around Virginia's fragile frame, and to protect her from all the elements that threatened to contaminate her pure life. She aroused a peculiar, protective, paternalistic feeling in me which at times caused me to experience a great inadequacy because I could not at any moment be everything and do everything for her.

I could continue expatiating on the state of amorous flux I found myself in for that petite mulatto. But the entrance of Major Piecemeal into the tent broke my pleasant contemplation. He greeted me with a nod, and seeing the lack of deference on Sam's part, kicked him, and told him to stand in the presence of an officer. Sam, hurt by the kick like an elephant would be from the nudge of a beetle, looked at me with his incessant eyes and his dull face. At my nod he lumbered to stand and retreated quietly into the shadows.

"If there is one thing that you will learn here," Piecemeal said haughtily to me, "is that slaves know their place. I do not know fully by what manner you have spoiled the niggers on your farm, but here you will learn—you must learn—that such an injustice will not be tolerated."

"Injustice?" I asked confused.

"Yes, sir, injustice. It is an injustice to you as a white man and an officer to elevate or otherwise treat your slaves as your equals, when they are clearly not so and never will be; and it is an injustice to the slaves to be treated in such a manner unbecoming of their positions and resulting only in an unwarranted pride and insolence."

"I marvel at your reasoning."

The Major laughed. "You northerners—what do you know of our society? You sit smug in your homes in New England or in your cabins in the plains and produce the vilest and most unfounded denunciations of a people you know nothing about, of a way of life you have not experienced, of an economic system foreign to your corrupt industry. And in the same breath you pity the negro, who in your own cities, even in his freedom, is the primary cause of crime and degradation. It is only when you deal with niggers day in and day out, when you witness their slothfulness, their avarice, their ignorance, their proclivity to violence, mayhem and every disorder, that you see why the race was doomed to forever be under the feet of the white man. That rule stands as firm today as when Noah first pronounced it.

"You refer to Noah's curse on Ham?"

"Certainly."

"I have reason to doubt your exegesis."

"It is not my interpretation, but that of our most learned divines. I marvel that you, an educated man, especially after having lived in our society for some time and seen those things of which I speak, debase yourself by your love for the negro."

If I had not known any better, I would have been led to believe that the Major had secret knowledge of my passions.

"Yes," I said deliberately; "I truly love the negro."

"Pshaw, sir," he said. "Do not even say such in jest. So far no one knows of your disposition, and I advise you to maintain this ignorance among us for your personal safety."

"Speaking of safety," said I, "do you intend to maintain this guard over me forever?"

"No, not forever. It would be inappropriate to have a commander lead his men into battle while he himself needs to be guarded. The guard will be lifted as soon as you realize the consequences of any lack of cooperation."

"And what is that? Do you threaten me again with imprisonment?"

"No, not that. In the military, treasonous acts are usually merited with execution."

"And are there not other men in Orleans more worthy than I of such foul treatment?" said I, indignant at my helplessness. "What have I done but come hither to see about my sick father, find him dead, inherit his estate, and then do with my property as I wish? Do you not do the same? Is there anyone who instructs you about your land or possessions? Is this not the United States?"

I caught my error too late, and my superior pounced on it.

"You find yourself altogether too attached to your section. Let me remind you that you are no longer in the United States, but in the Confederate States. The laws of your section afford you no protection here."

"You speak so proudly of your nation that I almost wish I had gray cloth covering my body," said I with sarcasm.

"Your desire shall not long remain unfulfilled. To-morrow you will visit the quartermaster and receive from him the vestments and equipment you will need. Then you will meet with me and the other officers to begin your training."

"When will I enter my command?"

"As soon as you are ready, you will go to the general camp and organize your men. Your love for the lowly will no doubt facilitate intercourse with the lot entrusted you."

ELEVEN

MY LOYALTY IS ACCEPTED

Our brigade consisted of three regiments. Lieutenant-Colonel Oak and his adjutant commanded ours, and I was placed over Company G. More than two thirds of my men were low-born and illiterate, coming from Mississippi and some of the poorest parishes in Louisiana. From among the more educated, some the sons of planters, I chose my lieutenants and sergeants. The name of my first lieutenant was Alfred Hartrey, a young man of twenty-two with a rich, brown complexion, and glossy, black hair that streaked abundantly behind his ears. His father owned a prosperous estate in Bertrandville and had planned for his son to go to Yale before the war began. He offered to buy the boy a substitute to enlist for him, but Alfred refused. The romantic glory of war washed over him, as it overran the countryside and enticed even the meanest to run, some without stockings or shoes, to the nearest draft table. Such is the opiate of adventure. One does not think of the blood, the slaughter, the destruction. All the horrid details one hid behind a pleasant mirage of iridescent lights, bombastic shouts, surges of inexplicable courage, valiant but deadly contestations of power, and the praises of maidens back home From high to low, all shake the hand of war, if by it they gain the glory of the sword and honor among peers.

To the excitement I too fell prey. To shape a group of one hundred straggling strangers into a cohesive colony of human ants that move and act all alike according to my commands was both a thrill and an exertion, particularly when I myself was as unlearned as they. It took two months until my company was ready to report to Lieutenant-Colonel Oak, who reviewed satisfactorily the drills with his good eye and admitted us into the regiment. I had so much proved my loyalty that I was at last given a sidearm and a sword (for the first month I was the only officer without arms) and was admitted into the general fellowship of the other commanders. Sam was given a small tent next to mine to dwell in, and the faithful negro was my attendant night and day. Whenever I needed a thing, he was there to provide it, even if it was only his comforting presence to remind me of what grew to be my new home. The other negroes in the camp often chided him for his intense devotion, but their opinion never swayed him or made him forget my past kindnesses to him and his family.

Having little knowledge of the military to begin with, I marveled that most of the other officers were as uninstructed as I. Of our group only Lieutenant-Colonel Oak had seen real action in the Mexican War, and his adjutant served merely at some outposts in guard against the indians. The other captains were as green as I, and little less green than the men they were over. Richard Taylor, in command of the 9th Louisiana, and who was to achieve some honor in the war, came to us and for a time oversaw our instruction. He was a decent and honorable man, and from him I learned the most of how to effectively manage a troop. Add to his tuition, my own background and experience managing a business, and I would have become (I speak as a fool), if my heart had been in it, a great Confederate commander. What a shame for my superiors that all the time I was learning with my hands to serve them, my mind was plotting to desert them.

Most of my men, as I have stated, were a ragged bunch, and their condition was hardly improved by the scant supplies distributed by the quartermaster. Shoes were in short supply and caused problems on long marches when the men had no shoes to begin with. But they were in such an excitable and impressionable state that the privations of army life did not immediately affect them. They were like children, thrust into some new experience, who do not rest day or night until every possibility is investigated and every uncertainty overcome. Owing to my position, I was quite comfortable in terms of shelter and necessities, but all of my machinations made me forget to be thankful and to curse even my passable situation.

Of necessity I ceased to write letters to Frederick. But every night I wrote him and my daughters epistles on my heart and prayed for their well-being. Whatever happened, they would be safe from the ravages of war. Any fighting would occur where I was, in enemy territory and even if the fighting shifted north, it, in all probability, would never reach New York. It was the North that was on the offensive. The South needed go nowhere but stand its ground and fight on its own soil. But how I missed my sweet, dimpled, offspring as I sat forlorn in my tent in the night, while afar off some musician played dirges on a pipe! They were perfect moments of reflection, and my mind never ceased its ruminations. It was then that I began to keep a journal, and the entries that survived I will include in this narrative where appropriate; where its original contents will serve my purpose better should my mind falter in its recollection, or should those recollections be inferior to their primary impressions.

To Mrs. Roget I wrote periodically. Her first response to me I read with trepidation, lest knowledge of my disrespect was exposed to her also, making me an object of her scorn. But there was no hint from her that she knew what had happened between Virginia and I. But, truly, I was sure all along that my sweet angel had not breathed a word to tarnish my name. Such was my hope in her sincerity and virtue.

The estate continued to operate well, without a hitch, under the supervision of Antoine and Mrs. Roget. Despite my suspicions about his character, Antoine was an extremely acute and capable fellow who learned the business well under my father. I continued to explicitly instruct Mrs. Roget as to the treatment of the slaves, especially Virginia; and of her cooperation I had no worry. She seemed to have softened greatly since I first arrived, and I counted her as a partner in my endeavors.

Of Virginia I inquired once, and received the response that she was well and still serving faithfully at the house. I could almost imagine her serving dinner, in silence, her elegant face, blessed with the soft features of our race, intent and assiduous.

And so I watched and planned and watched some more for my opportunity to escape my forced labor and involuntary imprisonment.

TWELVE

A TASTE OF WAR

W ithin the month my company, along with two others, were sent out on picket. Our headquarters turned out to be much better than I anticipated: an old, deserted plantation house, with one large parlor, a dining-room and several bedrooms. I shared one of the upstairs rooms with another captain. It was quite a comfortable situation, for the room contained a stove whose pipe went straight out a broken window. But because the stove often smoked the wrong way, we were forced to take refuge from the night chill in the parlor, which had an immense fireplace and bright fire. In the mornings, breakfast was served in the dining-room, hearty servings of eggs, sausages and biscuits. Then the morning reports began to arrive, a mounted officer or courier coming in from the general camp or some other place. I was outside in the piazza when a scout Piecemeal had sent out a fortnight ago reported that Union troops were crossing Mississippi on their way to the Pearl River. Because the entire state was virtually a battleground, it was in need of any available units to come to her defense. The command was given to vacate our pleasant hotel at dawn. The men were excited to say the least, as they looked forward to the opportunity of finally seeing some action. My thoughts were much less enthusiastic, except for the idea that perhaps I might surrender myself to the advancing Union troops and escape my predicament. Such a precarious decision had to be carefully mulled, for I had no intention of being caught between Scylla and Charybdis.

At daybreak, while the night's cold still lingered, we packed up our equipment and began our long march to Mississippi. Sam was compelled to ride in the back of our column, along with the other slaves and the provisions trucks. I sorely missed his company, but he was rather pleased at his propinquity to the "tasty vittles." Having a horse to convey me to our destination made the march not unpleasant. I felt badly, however, for some of my men, who, without the benefit of shoes, were forced to walk upon the terrain barefoot. Some commented that the only reason they would kill should the need arise was to come into the possession of some shoes.

Our trek took us through various homesteads. Slaves, particularly children, would climb fences and watch us as we passed, much like spectators at a parade. The younger men of my company, I soon found, at least those who came from families too poor to own slaves and who farmed their own land, were quite indifferent to the negroes. Some rather envied them in this particular instant where the men had to endure the trials of military life while the slaves remained better fed and secured on their plantations.

At noonday we were confronted by brackish marsh which seemed well nigh impenetrable at first glance. But we plodded through as best we could, losing some wagons along the way, their wooden wheels breaking from the exertion against the mud and tall weeds. It took us several hours to cross the short expanse of swamp, bringing us to the environs of the Pearl River, which served as a natural border between Louisiana and Mississippi. We proceeded up-river a way, in an attempt to locate a good place to ford it. The spot we found allowed our horses to wade through the water up to their shanks.

We were all exhausted by the time we arrived at the other side, and after another three mile march we stopped to rest in a field of tall grass. The air was still cool, but the sun warmed our weary faces. The men went about picking cranberries from bushes in a nearby grove. I stood looking out to the blue-ridged mountains in the distant north, wondering how soon we would meet with the offensive. Piecemeal guessed we would engage by the morn if we continued at our pace.

When the command was given, we again took up our accoutrements and continued. Although the spirits of my men seemed to heighten with each mile of southern ground we traversed, my own grew morose. The thought struck me, strangely enough for the first time, that there existed the marked possibility I should perish in battle. The manner of my death, whether at the end of a bayonet or under a hail of bullets, did not concern me. What made me shudder was the thought of all I was to leave behind. There was as yet a great deal of unfinished business in my life. I fancied the premature end of an unfulfilled life to be the most profoundly horrifying idea imaginable. I'd often wondered what thoughts were wont to cross a man's mind at that final, dread hour of judgment. Some say one's life flashes before the eyes. One's past life, however, cannot be changed. What is done is done. But the future, what can yet be done, carries with it the greater sorrow of inaction. I would not see my daughters grow and blossom like the springtime lilies. I would not see my business expand into ever increasing economic opportunities. I would never again see Virginia. For I knew that when that day came, when age and health would fail her, she would go to such a place where sorrows have ceased and all souls are warmed by the face of the Deity. But betwixt me and her there would be a great gulf, which no man can cross, and in my place I would cry out for her to but dip the tip of her finger in water to cool my tongue. But even then, while I suffer my sins, I would rejoice to see her lying in Abraham's bosom, sweet Virginia, and with no one to forbid her doing so.

We stopped our march when it turned dark, and camped in a wood. Before daybreak, we assembled and continued. The sounds of missiles, muffled by trees and distance, faint at first, began to sound hollowly in our ears. We knew an artillery battle was waging not three miles from whence we were. A scout reported spotting a new regiment of Union soldiers on their way to join the much larger Union force traversing the state. Since the 23rd Louisiana, with its assortment of howitzers, was also on the march, our mission then became to intercept the new regiment.

The relative peace of the shady wood, resounding with the jingle of tin cups the men hung from their rucksacks, seemed incongruous with our deadly march. I rode listlessly, letting my horse guide itself over the batches and fallen limbs. Virginia still hung heavy on my thoughts. If she did not love me as I loved her, I could not compel her. The affairs of the heart seem designed cruelly, a source of continual suffering for those not initiated into its mysteries. With Madeline, I had already tasted the sweetest happiness allowed a human being. I was a fool to think heaven would smile twice upon a man like me. My men—impressionable, wide-eyed youths—these men, though I had no love for their cause, stirred pity in me. For many, this expedition proved the first time they'd left their homes and families. It was these youths who deserved happiness, not I. To them would come wives and children and homes—if they lived.

We were ever aware of the possibility of snipers' bullets. It was my constant fear to be struck by a missile in a limb, or in the eyes, and thus endure the rest of my life as a living death. I preferred, should it come to that, to be pierced instantly through the heart. A sudden, hopefully painless death was at that moment perversely delightful.

Our forward line, of which I was part, stopped abruptly at the sound and sight of two scouts who came scurrying toward us through the wood. Major Piecemeal conferred with them briefly and then called the officers into a meeting. He explained the Union regiment was not but a mile from us, marching in a westerly direction. He then called for the assembly of three companies for a frontal assault. Mine was not among those he chose, and my spirits somewhat lifted as I hoped he wanted us to remain in the rear. But before I could lift my eyes in thanks, he drew apart to the shade of a mulberry tree and called me to him.

"It is my intention to cut off the Yankees head on," he explained to me. "But we are in need of a diversion. I would like you to take your company as far south and west as necessary, so that, when the regiment engages the larger element, you may attack on the flank in a feint. These Yankees will not retreat on southern soil, and if they do, you will be there to smash their rearward."

I was quite surprised at this proposition. He could have chosen to keep me with the larger body so as to maintain his supervision.

"Major," I said, finding the parlance of forced military courtesy uncomfortable, but, in the current context, necessary. "I perceive you are placing greater trust and faith in me than is perhaps warranted."

"Do not question me, Roget," said he. "I trust you no more than I would a prisoner, which you no doubt at this very moment consider yourself. But I am confident that you are an educated man, and in that light are conscious that any calculated misstep at this juncture will result in the most egregious of consequences. You will take your men to the rear of the enemy regiment and will attack them with the same ferocity as if they were about to pillage your very own home and hearth. If not, you will soon find yourself remaining permanently in this land, without, at worst, even the decency of a proper burial."

Piecemeal's words weighed heavily on me. Not only was I being forced to act against my will, but I was being ordered now to attack, maim and kill soldiers for whose cause I had an undoubtable sympathy. But the present objective, in hindsight, proved nothing to the greater misfortunes that would soon follow.

"I will do as you say," said I.

"Of course," Piecemeal said, a gleam of perverse satisfaction in his eye. "Once they are crushed or run off, we will meet again and this night celebrate our victory. I have brought with me an exquisite bottle of spiced rum which I will not be niggardly in sharing."

I took my leave without a nod or word, but he called me back.

"I think you have found your calling," he laughed. "Is not this a grand life?"

I stared at him, suddenly noticing how hot it was and how heavy my sword and scabbard hung at my side. I went back to my men and called the sergeant-major, whom I briefed on our sullen work. We soon took leave of the larger body, they going to their grim task, and we to ours.

After the larger body had amassed and noisily departed, my men became especially loquacious, presciently discussing the imminent exploits they would undergo on this their first real battle. We marched for an hour, slowly and deliberately, hampered by the random placement of trees, meandering rivulets and gutted ruts. But the time seemed much longer to me, for as I plodded on my mount, I took the leisure to notice every tree, every leaf, every rock, the intensity of every ray of sunlight that broke through the leafy canopy o'erhead. I wondered then what it was that went through the mind of a condemned man led to the gallows.

My senses seemed heightened. I could decipher the myriad conversations that occurred around me as if each was my particular interest. I saw simple men, farmers and yokels, many without shoes and most with their own weapons, arms which in happier times proved useful for nothing more than hunting small game. Their uniforms were laughable. Most wore the same clothes in which they enlisted. Sundry straw hats or woolen caps covered almost every head.

These men had nothing to fight for. They were little more than slaves themselves. They fought for an ephemeral glory, the glory of their South. My men did not know the nature of my position. To them I was part of that exalted class to which simple men find themselves in natural deference. I seemed what each aspired to: a wealthy, land-owing slaveholder. And I did nothing to dispel their illusion, for any dissension would have surely spelled an earlier woe for me.

Had I been in a less philosophical mood, I would have early noticed that, from a hillock, we were being tracked by a Union sniper. I noticed our guest too late, for as we waded a stream the cackle of gunfire took us by surprise. Immediately, one of the men to my right fell. I yelled to take cover, and the rest scampered to the brush to hide behind thick oaks and maples. My horse, frightened by the cacophony of violence, reared lustfully, nearly casting me off. But I managed to maintain control and steered the beast toward a defile shaded by old hickories whose long and bent branches nearly brushed the ground. There I dismounted, struck my beast upon its flank to shoo it away, and took cover behind the wood. With my revolver in hand I peered out warily, half expecting a round to strike my head. The men wrangled over secure positions behind trees. The whole wood, which only a minute before was alive with the whistle of birds and the rustle of leaves, fell into a deadly silence. Then I saw them, a blue wall materializing out of the tree line. My first impression was that Piecemeal had miscalculated his strategy, and that the whole brunt of the regiment was now against us. Whatever the case, there was precious little time to act. The dark-hued mass of the enemy stood six deep for at least thirty yards abreast. They began to form into a standard fusilade formation, where those in front take a knee so as to allow their comrades a clear view of fire. I called my men to assemble in like manner. Though we had drilled a hundred times, the rebels were pitiably disorganized, rushing about like rats colliding in a trap. I yelled until I was hoarse, and then only did the men take semblance of a formation.

The temptation to flee was strong in me. I thought of dashing across the wood into the Union fold. But I knew that I would probably be shot ere I took a step from my refuge. I also thought of surrendering my men, but such an act, I knew, would cause them to turn on me. With great reluctance I drew my saber, raised it, watched the flicker of its cruel gleam. I saw a commander on the other side do the same. What a game this was, I realized. We were all pawns trying to corner an imaginary king. My men glanced at me nervously, then at their enemy, then at me again. For a moment I loved them, and wished none to perish. Whether my arm fell before the Union fired upon us or after, I do not rightly remember. What is certain is that there occurred a near-simultaneous exchange of fire. In seconds the wood was so thick with black smoke that a man was fortunate if he could see five feet ahead of him. I fired also, emptying my revolver into wind. The cackle of gunfire persisted almost interminably while I reloaded and reloaded again. Stopping to check my person, mystified that nothing had pierced me in this rain of crisscrossing lead, I ordered my men to load their weapons anew.

The other side busied themselves also in sliding ram-rods into rifle-barrels. In seconds both armies fired upon each other again. Through the mists I could see my men falling. One second a man was standing upright, his eye at his rifle; and the next he crumpled onto the ground like a falling branch. Pitiable groans and shouts now filled the wood. I crawled over to one lad who was pierced in the belly. He sat against a tree still clutching his rifle, unable to speak. I looked into his eyes and a thousand horrors filled my mind. Never had I seen unadulterated death in such proximity. My Madeleine's passing was but a gentle trip from this world to the next, and she faded from me whilst I held her hand, a pleasant smile upon her lips. But this lad's countenance was twisted in an excruciating agony, and his inability to communicate the depths of his pain made his passion more complete. In the next instance his face dropped and all life snapped out of him.

"Sah, they'se ready to charge!" a breathless color-sergeant distracted me from my macabre contemplation. I looked out and saw, through the clouds, the blue wall advancing toward us. I called to Lieutenant Hartrey and ordered him to amass the men. Those who could still stand on two legs came running from whence they had scattered. When my force was largely reconstituted, I raised my sword among them and urged the attack in a swell of misplaced pride. Ere I could take a step, the men swept by me, almost impaling me in the process on their bayonets. The dreaded rebel yell, a sound I had heard only in nascent form throughout our many drills, now surged through my ragtag company like a minor swell that quickly, by force of wind and water, becomes a crashing wave. It was a noise that could not be approximated by the more urbane Northerners, for it arose out of the very earth. It was a cry that was later sensationalized in *Harper's Weekly* as a guttural, primeval noise that could freeze men in their tracks. In this, the journal was not too far amiss, for I felt a shiver pass through my body as the crescendo increased, until it seemed the men were possessed of some bacchanalic frenzy.

The heavy fog of gunsmoke prevented me from seeing much of the action ahead, but I heard the clash of arms and the sounds of embattled fury. There was then complete and utter pandemonium. Men, both gray and blue, ran to and fro. They fought all around me, hand to hand, some as concrete bodies, others in the form of abstract shadows.

I felt a tremendous fear, so much so that I was unable to move. It was more than a fear of dying violently; it was a dread born from my own loneliness and insignificance. Every man, particularly a man of my estate, fancies himself in possession of the world. In civilized society he has a certain measure of control over the quality of his life. He eats well, lives comfortably and fears no man. Thoughts of mortality, that ever present and eternal chaos consistently impinging on our ordered lives, seem afar off. There is a rhyme and reason to life, an order, a discipline. But that illusion is quickly shattered when the man finds himself in a lonely wood, friendless and powerless, in the midst of a deadly struggle for existence. He could be the most devout of all religious men, but his faith will not save him from imminent death. I could not help but think of the Savior's pitiable cry before his last gasp upon the tree of crucifixion: "My God, My God, why have you forsaken me?" It is that utter, senseless, cruel loneliness while teetering on the edge of oblivion that is perhaps unparalleled in the horrors to which fate has subjected wretched mankind.

The whole melee, in retrospect, now seems like a far-off dream. I cannot now say with certainty for how long I stood motionless while men died around me. The precision with which my senses were imbued was startling—a worthy subject of study for physiologists. I could smell every atom of blood, see the wobbly flight of lead and hear the leaves scrunched underfoot as men ran or fell. But thankfully, this state of suspended animation did not prevent me from reacting to a Union soldier who materialized out of the gloom and charged at me with his bayonet. When he was yet three yards from me I discharged my revolver. One shot halted him momentarily, and then another permanently arrested his advance, knocking him off his feet and onto his back. Such an act of mortal immediacy brought my senses squarely back into reality, and I realized again where I was. Lieutenant Hartrey came running, his shoulder bloodied, and grasped me like a drunkard seeking support. He was breathless and not even the exertion could restore a semblance of natural color to his pale, frightened face streaked with black powder.

"We can't sir," he shouted. "It's not possible...too many...we must retreat."

I looked behind him at the dead bodies strewn across the clearing. The man I had just killed still lay where he fell. I was able to recognize many of my men, unless they were mutilated or lying face down in death. From what I could determine, my company was locked in a hopeless battle. I knew I had to move to the rear, whatever was left of it, find the bugle boy if he was still alive, and have him sound a retreat. But before I could embark on this last effort to save whatever of my troop was left, a fresh noise sounded in the distance. Within minutes the balance of the regiment entered the fracas, precisely as my company was to do had the original formulation gone as planned. The influx of new bodies allowed me to pull Hartrey, who weakened with every moment, to the rear. When he could go no more I sat him among the gnarly roots of an old maple and examined his wound. It was not deep, but the loss of blood, however minimal, coupled with the exertion and excitement of battle, no doubt ill-affected his constituency.

I remained with Hartrey for the remainder of the skirmish, which was not long in concluding. Our force succeeded in completely routing the Union regiment. Upward of an hundred and fifty men died from both sides. It was my company who suffered the greatest casualties, not counting the wounded.

We captured over fifty Union prisoners, who were entrusted to B Company for safekeeping. The men under my command, those who could walk, came straggling back to me, weary, but some with strange, exhilarated countenances. It would have been more appropriate for the Greeks to have made Janus their god of war, for the two faces of battle exist simultaneously in a paradoxical collusion. Some men meet their untimely end; the rest reminisce like the whole thing was one grand sport.

Back at the camp, I entrusted Hartrey to the surgeons and was met by Sam on my way back to my tent. The faithful negro gave me such an embrace that he lifted me clear off my feet as if I was a bale of cotton. He would have kissed me also, had I not backed away, trying delicately not to offend his generous enthusiasm.

"Oh, Mas'r Roget, I'se so glad t'see you'se alibe and well," he said. "I wuz here a'pacin' back en fo'th, back en fo'th, prayin' that no harm wood come t'you."

"I thank Providence," I said, tempted to engage Sam in a philosophical discussion of why I lived while others perished. But at that very moment Major Piecemeal rode up to us on horseback. Sam stepped away deferentially.

"If there is one thing you will learn in war," he said, removing his gloves and patting the dust from his shoulders: "it is to always expect the unexpected."

"And incompetence as well," said I.

"You've done well, Roget," Piecemeal said with a forced smile. "You may persuade me yet to place further trust in you."

With this he reared his horse and trotted away.

THIRTEEN

MY FIRST ESCAPE

The far away cries of brethren, locked in battle and death, did not dampen the enthusiasm and revelry with which the soldiers welcomed the coming of fall. Despite minor skirmishes, the Mississippi had not yet become the crucial thoroughfare for the South's destruction. Emboldened by recent victory, there was a sense of safety and inviolability throughout the camp, and the men had the impression that the military life, apart from the cumbersome daily drills, was one of leisure and friendly fellowship in the midst of exciting battles. Those young men had received only a taste of the tremendous strain the war was to put on their humanity in the years to come.

One night, at the arrival of a large contingent of Mississippi troops, senior officers issued three casks of spirits per company, and, tin cups in hand, the men lined up to eagerly join the celebration. Much music sounded throughout the whole camp: drums, pipes, and an occasional horn. After an officer's meeting, in which we were briefed as to events in Virginia, I returned to my tent and there endured the noise which robbed me of my sleep through most of the night. Several times, my own men came to see me that I might be arbiter in some grievance among them caused through drunken inconsideration. I did my best to understand the intoxicated babble which made their southern solecisms even more peculiar. Then I pronounced judgment and sent them on, wishing only to be left alone to sleep. The music, accompanied by celebratory rifle cracks, continued for most of the night, so that by early morning, when I awoke suddenly, I was surprised at the quiet.

Sam was kneeling by my bed, his large face in front of mine. I shook in sudden fright at the sight of his black countenance, at first unfamiliar in those confused first few seconds that follow awakening. It was still fairly dark outside, and the light of the lamp which Sam held over his head caused sinister shadows around his protruding features. His face shone with perspiration, and his eyes drilled intently into mine.

"Mas'r, you 'wake?"

"Yes, Sam," I responded. "What is the matter?"

"Diden you tell me to keep my eyes up an' tell you if I sees sumthing'?"

"Yes, what—"

"Mas'r, mos' ob de people in de camp is drunk on 'ccount of knockin' de jug so much all thru de night. You could hear dem snoring' in ebery place. The sun's 'most up, won't be but 'nother hour or so, and it's a good time, right now, to 'scape."

I had made Sam my confidant in my plans, and had asked him to be my eyes and ears. The slaves of a plantation usually know more about what is happening at the plantation than the owners. It was the same at the camp.

The negroes who were kept as laborers, teamsters, and cooks formed an intelligence committee, and though the officers tried to keep them ignorant, knew about as much as they concerning even insignificant skirmishes. Sam quickly became accepted among them and informed me of much that was happening outside the Confederacy, some of which was unknown even to the officers at the camp. For example, I learned that the Union was planning to take New Orleans by way of the outlet of the Mississippi into the Gulf of Mexico. I spoke to Major Piecemeal about the possibility, and after declaring that he had heard no such thing, proceeded to show me the impossibility of such an attack because Forts Jackson and St. Philip created an impenetrable bottleneck in defense of the city, and only an attack from the north down the river would have any chance of success. To my satisfaction, I learned three months later, while in prison, of the taking of New Orleans by the very means described to me by Sam from his able informants.

"Do you think so, Sam? Do you think now is a good time?" I asked him.

"Mos' surely. Eben de pickets is asleep. I'se seen dem. Dere's two at de no'th side ob de camp and dey's asleep in each other's arms like two li'l babes. I 'most laughed when I saw dem, but I held it in 'cause I didn't want to wake dem up."

"But I feel unprepared to go now."

"Don't matter none, Mas'r. You don't need much preparin'. Did you think you was going to take all dem bags wid you? There ain't no way you can 'scape dat way. You take it from me. I'se seen nigger's 'scape all de time. Dose that took all de truck dey had was caught right fast. You jus' got to git up and go."

I jumped from my bed and pulled my head into the cold air outside. It took a moment for my eyes to adjust, and to see the white eyes and teeth of half a dozen negroes who were sitting and squatting outside my tent. They smiled at me and nodded. I did the same and brought my head back inside.

"What are they doing out there?" I asked Sam.

"Dey's my frends, Mas'r. Dey's gonna help us get out ob dis place."

"You told them of me?"

"Sho'. But you don't got to worry 'bout dem. They know you'se from de No'th an' I tol' dem how good a Mas'r you was and how you tol' us we wasn't slaves no mo' and paid us money as if we was free and workin'. Dey's good niggers, all ob dem, and dey's gonna help us."

Being as a good a time as any to escape, I bundled a few articles of clothing in my haversack, loaded my gun, took my journal, and followed Sam outside. The negroes stood when I appeared. I recognized one, a brown fellow with a withered hand who drove the rations wagon through the camp. Another handed Sam a small bundle wrapped in rope. I drew up the buttons of my coat, and turned myself over to my sable guardians. Sam gave an order and all of the negroes save the teamster disappeared into the camp. Already I could discern the tents on the eastern side, like a multitude of little hills, as the sky began to brighten

"Dis here's Crispus. He knows dis place like de back ob his good hand," Sam, introduced me to the man.

"Yes, sah," Crispus said. "I'll lead you out ob here mos' ob de way, 'specially thru de swamp, 'cause I think dat's de bes' way to go. Den I'll show you where to go from dere. Come on."

With Sam behind me I followed Crispus. The other negroes had gone out to watch, Sam informed me, as sentinels in strategic positions about the camp. Should our flight be in jeopardy, certain animal calls would serve as a warning. And so at the howling of a coyote, Sam dragged me down behind a tent and covered my mouth with his hand. Of course, it was not a coyote making noise, but one of the negroes. At the bark of a dog, we proceeded again.

At the edge of the camp lay a cypress swamp that led nearly to the Pontchartrain. We made our way carefully through the maze of tents, wanting to clear the camp before sunrise, when it was certain that some of the men would begin to awake.

The jagged edges of the cypress-trees came into sight, when, passing a tent, we came face to face with one of my very own men. His hair was in disarray and he was rubbing his eyes. We stopped dead in our tracks at this discovery and I grew afraid. But I remembered my relationship to him and spoke gently.

"What are you doing up, Jameson?"

To my relief, the lad, only sixteen, seemed not at all suspicious of me or my comrades. He yawned and rubbed his eyes more.

"Nothing t'all, Cap'n. Just got to get rid of some of that bark juice I had last night."

I laughed felicitously and patted him on the shoulder. He went behind his tent to do his business and we proceeded to ours.

By sunrise we entered the swamp. The roots of the trees and the thickets covering the ground made the walk arduous; but Crispus led us as best as he could. Soon, we were surrounded by trees and the camp seemed very far behind us. At one point, I slipped on a mossy log and fell into the muddy foliage. Sam picked me up and brushed me off in rough strokes.

We trod for an hour when Crispus suddenly stopped and bade us to be silent. I looked about me and concentrated on the acuity of my hearing. But all that reached them was the sound of a stream ahead of us, and the rustling of the leaves.

"Dey's comin'," Sam whispered.

"Are they following us?" I asked.

"Yes," Crispus said. "Don't know how, but dey's comin'."

We took off in an easterly direction. As we approached the stream, the ground becoming so wet that my boots sunk neatly in it, leaving very conspicuous prints, I now heard the dogs and the crash of branches. My heart race as we quickened our pace, the poor Crispus balancing himself over difficult terrain with his one good hand out-stretched, the other bouncing lifelessly against his belly. I turned my head continuously to see what was happening behind us, but since I was running, all I witnessed was an indiscernible green and brown blur about me. All of a sudden, I heard shouts and the crack of a rifle. I looked back to see Sam fall into the foliage as two large black bloodhounds come bounding toward me. I scampered quickly up a log that was leaning against a stunted tree. Wildly, I reached for the branches and pulled myself up, in time to feel the bite of one of the hounds against by heel. A swift kick stalled the beast while I pulled myself up to safety. From my position, I saw Sam sitting on the ground, his arm bleeding, three soldiers on horseback, and one of the hounds on top of Crispus. With my pistol I took aim and grazed that dog across the head, sending it yelping away The noise made my own beast cautious, and it stood back, looking up at me and growling. Crispus was bitten on the shoulder and he wearily pulled himself up on the log. I aimed my gun at the closest horseman and then saw it was my own lieutenant, Alfred Hartrey. Behind him were two of my men, their rifles trained nervously on me. Alfred waved his hand, and the boys, to their relief, lowered their rifles.

"Good morning, Captain. I reckon it's a fine time for a walk 'round this way," Alfred said, smiling.

"Yes," I said. "This is a lovely swamp."

"Captain, why don't you put that there gun down?"

I lowered it slowly, and seeing no use for it, placed it in my coat pocket.

"These men need medical attention," I said.

"Don't know if they'll get it. You better come along with us, Captain."

I looked at Sam, tightly clutching his arm, then came down from the tree. One of the hounds came toward me but was held at bay on its leash. The lieutenant pulled out his handkerchief and held it out for me. I took it and bound Sam's arm. Crispus was on his feet, the arm of his good hand bent awkwardly toward the same wounded shoulder. I went to look at the wound and found it was not very serious. Nevertheless, I put Crispus' arm around my shoulder and supported him.

The three of us walked slowly in front of our captors, I with my burden and Sam next to us. Alfred did not rush us, but allowed us to go at our tired pace, made even slower by our injuries.

"We were just following orders, Captain," Alfred said to me. "They told me to take the bloodhounds and come after you. I would've liked to have stayed in bed another half-hour if I could've helped it."

"Would you have shot me, Alfred?" I asked.

"No, sir. They told us there was some niggers with you, so that's why we brought the dogs. We wasn't sure what to expect. But we wouldn't have fired at you, would we?" he asked of the other boys, who swore they would not have done so.

"Now, Captain, if you don't mind me asking, what's this all about? You're helping these niggers to escape?"

"Rather," said I, "they were helping *me* to escape."

"What're you talking about, Captain?"

The rest of the way back to the camp, I explained to my captors the details of my situation. They were astounded and at one point one of the boys exclaimed, "Wall, dog-gone, he's a Yank!" while the other said, "T'aint that somethin'!"

We were met at the camp by astonished stares from men standing by their tents or peeking out of them, cooking by their fires, or simply milling about in their long coats. We were marched along the dewy grass of the main thoroughfare that wound through the camp from one end to the other. Major Piecemeal rode out to us on his bay, his face imprinted with a disconsolate weariness, and his eyes bloodshot. He reined in front of me and dismounted. I let Crispus to sit upon the ground.

"I expected this would happen sometime," Piecemeal said to me; then, with an outstretched arm, "Give me your gun."

From my pocket I extracted my pistol and placed it in his palm.

"I see the negroes are ever ready to give you aid," he said.

"These men are wounded," said I. "They must be cared for."

"Oh, they'll be cared for," he said and ordered two soldiers to take Sam and Crispus away. Crispus went tractably, but Sam raised himself to his full form and threatened them like a wary bear. He said to me, "Mas'r, I won't leave you." One of the soldiers menaced him with his bayonet, but Sam, with one swift swing of his arm, knocked him sprawling. I cried for him to comply when several soldiers rushed out and brought him down with blows. I tried to pull back some of the assailants, when Alfred, off from his horse, held me back forcefully. Sam was knocked without sense and led away. The sight of such a powerful man beaten elicited pathos, and I prayed silently for his safety.

"I said that man was wounded," I addressed Piecemeal.

"You make it all too difficult for yourself, Captain. You might as well cooperate fully with us now."

I was deposited inside a small tent containing only a cot. A detail was put around the tent, and food, in the form of fried bacon and hardtack, was brought to me. There I remained until the afternoon, when I was called before the officers for a court-martial.

Around noon, during my confinement, I heard a round of sharp rifle cracks. I thought nothing of it, imagining the noise to have been target practice among the soldiers. But I learned the shots were aimed at the hearts of Sam and Crispus. They were executed mercilessly and their bodies thrown into a ditch outside the camp.

FOURTEEN

JUDGMENT IS PASSED

Early the next morning, I did not need to be awakened. It would be a generous calculation to say that I slept three hours with the sentinels outside, inking ugly and grotesque shadows on my tent. The words of Major Piecemeal came often in my dreams, and I saw him as a ten-foot giant mercilessly condemning me to the care of the hangman. Between troubled naps I prayed for deliverance, that as Daniel was saved from the lion's den, or his friends from the furnace, I should be delivered from a cruel death at rebel hands. But it was strange that I was not more anxious than I was. Surely, a man who knew that he was probably going to die would find himself in deep despair, lamenting what he had failed to do in life, and what was left undone. But I had the feeling in me that I would not die. My two daughters would be left alone; for them alone I had to survive. I also wanted to take Virginia home, determined to do everything in my power to treat her well, to place her in opulence and ease, to satisfy her needs and fulfill her desires. At my home in New York, she would have all she needed. Yes, we would sit and face the Hudson on the early mornings, its blue water lapping tenderly against the cliffside, and the sun beginning to warm our necks and hands. She could read to me from books (and how she will delight in my copious library) and I would delight in quizzing her sensitive mind. We would also take long walks through lonely Inwood, whose abundance of solitary paths afforded the luxury of isolation. The shady maples and tall pines, enveloping us in a world of living green, would shield us from the social chaos without. There Virginia would expatiate on her life and dreams to my listening ears. We would walk and talk and listen to the chirrups of the birds. The stoniest afflictions and sharpest grievances would become forgotten pinpricks in the cushion of charitous companionship.

Major Piecemeal was eating breakfast in his tent when I was brought before him. He bade me to sit down on a cracker-box and sent my guards to wait outside. He did not speak until I had watched him slice and eat his last bit of bacon.

"What should I do with you?" he asked calmly, as if I was an old friend come in for a chat.

"Set me free and allow me to return to my home," said I.

"That, Mr. Roget, I cannot do. There is no telling what type of mayhem you could begin."

"I assure you that I would do no such thing."

"You assured me you would be loyal."

"Would not you have done the same? A man cannot be held responsible for rebellion against injustice. I am a simple man, held against my will, with two children at home and an unwanted inheritance. I am a father, sir."

"And a spy."

"I am no spy."

"There were reports that you were arming your slaves."

"There is no truth in those reports."

"You deny them?"

"Without a doubt."

"And your escape, with the help of your negro, do you deny that?"

"No, of course not; but I did not plan the flight last night."

"What of the picket guards that were murdered?"

"Murdered?" I asked alarmed.

"Do not tell me you did not know of this."

"I did not," said I, grieved.

"They were found murdered, their throats cut, shortly after it was discovered that you were gone."

"I tell you no, sir. I had no knowledge of the murders. I would not have condoned them even if they meant my freedom."

"Your negro, then, acted on his own?"

"I regret to say it, but he must have—alone or in concert with others in the camp."

"What a faithful fellow! You have a great way with niggers, persuading them to attack even armed soldiers. I am impressed."

"If what you say is true, Sam acted entirely on his own. I am greatly saddened to hear of the deaths."

"Do not anger me with your affection. You are fortunate that you

are not, even now, lying in the same grave as your beloved niggers. Remember
I told you the penalty for treason? It is, I think, what you deserve. But my
superior is less hard-hearted than I and recommended that you be committed
to prison instead. Therefore, today you will be put on a train for Alabama, to
be sent to the prison in Cahaba, with the rest of you Yankee bastards."

The Major did not allow me to speak. The guards came in and took
me back to my tent, where I was ordered to pack my belongings in a sack.
Then I was driven on a cart to the nearest station, where, accompanied by four
soldiers, I was put on a train traveling north. My place was in a box car, amid
various supplies in large crates. There I lived until we reached Jackson,
Mississippi, where I was allowed to go outside and walk for five minutes.
From Jackson we took another train eastward. The train went south near
Selma, and we arrived, a day and a half later, at Cahaba.

FIFTEEN

I ENTER HELL

I t is with some trepidation that I begin this part of the narrative. To search my mind again for memories I had long since tried to bury has been a rather unpleasant chore. The memories of horror are always vivid, and once resurrected, become hard pressed to be laid to rest again. Since the times of the events I relate, several men on both sides have published excellent memoirs of their prison life during the war, exposing the extreme suffering and cruelty prevalent at the prisons. But their recollections are oftimes laced with a great sectional loyalty and a certain romanticism. In my case, my only loyalty was to myself and those I loved. Add to the corporal punishment I experienced at Cahaba the mental anguish of longing to see my children, as well as of my misdeed with Virginia and the consequent thought that I had lost her forever, intensified by the months of hopeless and agonizing torture, and it will be apparent how imprisonment for me proved a double curse.

The town of Cahaba lay five miles west of the Alabama river.   The prison, by the same name because of its close proximity, was two miles south. With about a hundred Union soldiers captured in battle, I was held in an abandoned tobacco warehouse converted into a temporary prison. Men were detained there daily on their way to the prison. Because of my gray uniform, which through cruelty was allowed to remain on me, the men in blue avoided me and gave me looks of contempt.   I therefore sought the company of a handful of Confederate traitors and deserters, not wishing to create problems by my incongruous identity. The Union soldiers encircled us and kept us at a distance from them, confined in a corner of the warehouse. When one of the Confederates proclaimed out loud his loyalty for the Union, a Union soldier came forward and shouted, "Lookit this grey back! He's a secesh one minit, an' a turncoat th' next. These damn secesh!"

We were confined to the warehouse overnight, receiving only two pieces of hardtack and water for dinner. Because I had not eaten since I left the camp, the coarse and tasteless cracker was welcome fare, and so I ate one heartily, putting the other piece in my pocket.

In the morning, about fifty prisoners, including myself, were marched outside in two squads. We were walked through the town and quickly became the center of attention, although the townspeople no doubt were accustomed to the same scene every day. Men and women came out of their homes and shops to observe the captured aggressors. Some had contempt and disparage on their faces, and their mouths opened to express their sentiments. Others possessed compelling looks of pity. Their sad faces expressed no partisanship, only a concern for men, who, despite their loyalties, were still men not much different from their sons, brothers, and husbands. Those who seemed the most empathetic were the women. They looked into our eyes and upon our condition with motherly concern.

Our squads were marched under guard the two miles to the prison.
The country was very hilly, and the first glimpse we received of the prison was
soon lost in the undulations of the terrain. But soon the structure became a
fixed object, growing ever larger, as my companions and myself grew more
morose. Our time at the tobacco warehouse was spent in speculation about
our destination, encouraged by those who seemed somewhere to have acquired
a certain knowledge of the prison, who assured us that we were heading to a
hell on earth, and that we would be fortunate to ever get out alive. Truly, at
such an early time, little was known of the prison systems employed by the two
sides. The public, enthused by accounts of daring battles, paid scant attention
to the fate of those captured in battle. These men simply disappeared. It was
not until later during the war, when journalists were allowed to examine the
prisons, that the public became fully aware of the horrors experienced by the
prisoners, men who would have gladly given their lives over and over again in
the most atrocious fighting than spend another day incarcerated under such
inhuman conditions.

We passed a tall guard post, at the top of which soldiers had their rifles
trained on us. The prison rose before us: a massive stockade of tree logs
measuring over a thousand and a half feet in length and nearly half that in
width. The main gate, situated like a triangle in the center of the west face,
dragged opened slowly and ponderously. More soldiers stood atop the
palisade, but none said a word. Once the gates were opened enough for us to
pass, we could see yet another palisade inside it, about sixty feet from the outer
one. Once inside and between the palisades, our squads were split. One went
south and mine went north, to a smaller gate on the inner palisade. When it
opened, we were met by soldiers holding back great Russian bloodhounds on
chains. But the dogs were not trained on us. They were trained on a multitude
of prisoners who crowded around the inside of the gate. They stood like
wraiths in shredded clothing, their thin, lanky bodies evidence of prodigious

malnourishment. There was not one man who was fully dressed. Many draped themselves with thread-bare blankets because of the cold. Others, without blankets, had shirts but no trousers. Some had trousers, but no shirts. Most still wore remnants of their kepis, with no brim and no crown, allowing their wildly growing hair to sprout out like too many flowers in too small a vase.

A great stench assailed us as we were ushered into the company of the wraiths and into a vast, undulating wasteland of tents, fires, and poles. The commander of our guard ordered us to spread out as far as possible from the gate to avoid congestion. The guards and the dogs were withdrawn and the gate was closed. We were left, bewildered, in the company of men we would at one time have embraced, but then avoided out of loathing for their pitiful conditions.

My gray coat brought me stares and scorn from the prisoners as I made my way through the tents and fires to a suitable place where I could situate myself. When I reached a point where all I could see in every direction were the billowing folds of tents, I set my sack down and sat on the ground. Despite my warm coat, I was miserably cold, and the wraith-like men who passed me by, exhaling white breath, were no comfort.

I sat in my spot for an hour, without fire or tent. After turning my coat inside out to display a darker lining, I walked to the nearest inmate. He was wrapped in a fraying blanket and was doubled over a fire on which he was cooking beans in a small, grease-encrusted pan. The handle had long fallen off, and so he held the rim of the pan by a rag, bringing the pan close to the fire without scorching his hand. He looked up as I approached, and moved the pan back from the fire. His face was grimed with dirt and soot, and his wet hair was matted like a filthy net upon his head.

"Fresh fish," he muttered irritably as I, uninvited, sat by him. When he had looked me over a minute longer, he turned back his attention to the cooking of his beans.

"Yes," I said. "I came in an hour ago."

"Bryant's my name," he said. "Yeh hungry?"

"Yes," said I, removing a piece of the hardtack we were served at the warehouse from my pocket, and beginning to eat it.

"It's good yeh got that tack. Rations ain't till noon, an' I ain't givin' yeh any of my beans."

Had he offered me some of his beans, I would have declined. It was not my desire to deprive any man of the dozen beans he intended to eat for breakfast.

"Tell me," I asked him. "Where can I get a tent?"

"Yeh don't got a tent?"

"No."

"Yeh better make one, then."

"With what?"

"With whatever yeh got."

I noticed that Bryant's tent was nothing more than two or three shirts, cut open and sewed together to make a large flap. It rested on a single pole and covered what seemed to be a hole in the ground. I peered in closer, and indeed it was a hole, large enough for a man to fit in.

"You sleep in the ground?" I asked.

"Yep, it's downright comf'table. Keeps yeh warm at night."

I contemplated the horrid notion that I would perhaps have to do the same, and like some ground-hog live in the earth. But I resolved that I would become terricolous only as a last resort, and that I would try to live simply within the confines of a small tent if I could make one.

When the beans were cooked, Bryant drained the water and began to eat them with his fingers. I looked through my sack to see out of what I could make a tent and soon discovered that I would need the sack itself. And so I ripped it apart at the seams until I had an adequate rectangular flap. All I needed was wood to make a frame, or at least a simple pole to hold it up.

"Are there any trees here?" I asked Bryant with the intention of procuring branches from them, not only for my tent, but as tinder for a fire.

"They're scarce as hens teeth," was his terse response.

I made my sack into a sack again, securing its corners with my hand, and started out in search of trees. I noticed how the ground was marked in many places with roots and furrows. Many small trees had existed in the area before the men cut them down.

A stream ran through the center of the stockade from east to west, the only source of water for the prison. But it was a foul stream, and a mire overgrown with weeds surrounded it. The mire emitted a disagreeable effluvium which alerted me to its presence even before I reached it. In that place did the prisoners bathe, wash their clothing, drink, and rid themselves of their waste. In my still healthy and sufficient state, I loathed the area. I had no idea that the stream would become for me, despite its turpid state, a source of happiness; it became for me a custom to journey every morning to the stream and to bathe my head and limbs. Without the daily refreshment, I would have surely atrophied and died, as many of my companions, who, finding no reason even to move, remained in their tents without water or nourishment for many days until, ineluctably, a lonesome death took them. But the walk to the stream, for me, was exercise, and the cool water against my skin revived me each day of my tenure.

I found no branches long enough to serve as a support for the tent I was intent on constructing. It seemed every tree that at one time lived in the stockade had been cut down. But I did secure some fire wood from tree stumps with the aid of a hand-axe that someone lent to me in exchange for some pieces of tack.

As I was returning to my station, a commotion began among the prisoners, and in a mass everyone moved toward the inner gate. I could do nothing less than go along to see what was the cause of the stir. The gate through which I first had entered swung in and soldiers, bayonets poised, entered the stockade. They made a passage for a negro driving a long cart piled high with foodstuffs. The prisoners seemed to have developed an organized way of distributing the daily rations. The procedure was led by a large German by the name of Bight Helhorn, who, I soon learned, was the equitable but uncompromising "police captain" of our area. The prisoners had organized an informal police force among themselves in order to deal with the "raiders" and "flankers"—names given to thieves and malefactors. If a flanker or raider was caught, Bight would hear the case, and then have his men mete out a proper punishment, which usually amounted to a severe beating. The custom later developed of shaving half the head and beard of a flanker, as a public mark of his sin. These poor individuals were sorely abused until their hair grew back. Stealing food was a very serious crime; and understandably so, for most of the men had not enough food to sustain themselves, much less being able to afford to have it stolen. The police force was necessary not only for the protection of the prisoners, but for the thieves themselves, whom at first were murdered by the mobs. When the Confederates who ran the prison discovered what was occurring, they encouraged the formation of the police force.

I stood in line to receive my ration, which amounted to two cupfuls of cornmeal and a cupful of beans. There were some rotten potatoes, but these soon ran out before I arrived at the cart. I lingered in the area, putting my rations in a pocket, and watched how the hill of food upon the cart slowly disappeared into the possession of the hungry prisoners. I was about to turn back to my place when a man beckoned to me to look in a certain direction. In that direction stood Bight, who, in an accented shout, demanded that I follow the cart to the side of the gate where lay a mound of corpses. These I did not notice when I had entered. The men who were appointed with me began to pick up the bodies, and to my horror, to pile them on the cart—the same cart in which our food was brought! Not wanting any part of the exercise, I began to back off when a rough hand grabbed me by the collar. I looked up into the red, rock-like face of Bight. With a curse, he pushed me roughly toward the bodies and I almost fell among them. Wishing to avoid any further confrontation, I grabbed the feet of one corpse while another grabbed the shoulders. We carried it to the cart and threw it in. To my further horror, being close enough to look into the cart, I saw that the bottom of it was covered with maggots. Again, I thought that our food came from that same cart! The procedure was not a unique occurrence on that day. Each day afterward the cart came in with food, and each day it went out with the dead. The cart was never cleaned, as far as I could tell. The maggots and filth lived equally well in the food and in the dead flesh of departed prisoners.

When all of the bodies were piled on the cart, almost naked bodies with no shoes or shirts or breeches (the living appropriated what the deceased no longer needed), the negro snapped his team and drove the cart out. The soldiers followed and the gate was shut. The prisoners returned to their normalcy. I stood sick with a nauseous sensation. In a daze I walked back to my place and lay on the cold ground with my blanket over me. There I tried to sleep. When I awoke, I remembered the food in my pockets and took it out. To my dismay, the cornmeal contained a few maggots and I cast it all from me. My appetite was no longer with me in any case.

For two days I ate nothing, not even bothering to get rations. My beans I buried in the ground under me. On the third day, my great hunger forced me to dig up the beans and to eat them, boiling them in a tin cup I had in my possession. I grew grateful for that tin cup, until it was stolen, for without it I could not cook my beans or my meal. On the third day, I stood in line for rations, receiving more maggot-infested meal and a few turnips. Dutifully I picked out the maggots and made a cake of the meal. I ate with such relish that I scarcely remembered better fare.

SIXTEEN

LIFE IN PRISON

The days grew colder and I hungrier and thinner. When my shoes were stolen, I was forced to walk barefoot. Since most of the men went about barefoot, I did not feel as sorry for myself. As long as I had my coat and my tin cup, I was consoled,

After two weeks I began again to write in my journal. Having lost my pencil, I wrote with a sharpened piece of charred wood. It was tremendously comforting to write and to reflect in words the thoughts that daily weighed on me. To write I had a great amount of time, since there was little to do but survive. Most of the day I spent sitting in my tent (after petitioning for wood, I and several other prisoners were allowed outside briefly to gather it. I was able to find enough branches to construct an adequate frame for the sack that served as my tent), or visiting other prisoners whom I had befriended. I have included here some of the entries that were preserved in my journal. Forgive me, reader, if the entries were written with a certain abandon, and without the conscientious literary ability employed in the rest of this narrative. When the mind is racked with anxiety, and the body afflicted with disease and famine, many powers fall into abeyance.

Jan. 26th—My clothes have became so torn and dirty that they have lost their Confederate character. I have became a Union soldier captured at the battle of Ball's Bluff in Virginia. My new identity makes me feel more comfortable among all of the Yankees. Interviewing a soldier also captured at that battle, I obtained all of the information I needed in case I was ever questioned, as well as for the frequent night-time war chats of the soldiers. I often have to use the little factual information I have, and commingle it with fantastic descriptions of my own imagination, in order to contribute my portion when my friends come together and recount the glories and failures of battles in which they were involved. Despite the wretched conditions they find themselves in, the men remain incredibly loyal to the Union and the cause of the North. They do not feel abandoned by their government, but have abiding hope in its faithfulness. News of victories on the battlefields, when it comes to their ears, elicit great joy and enthusiasm; while notices of defeat produce gloom and sadness. Rumors are ever going around that there is a Federal troop nearby, and that we are to be soon freed. A chaplain among us, Reverend Theodore Grayson, exhorts us continually to remain steadfast and patient for deliverance. We console ourselves continually in freedom, and we dream of home and hearths, of a warm bath, of a full and hearty meal.

Jan. 28th—Awakened early in the morning by shouts, I stuck my head out of my tent to see a man run before my face. He was soon followed by a mob. When they caught the flanker, a young red-haired man, they dragged him to the ground and commenced to kick him. Bight appeared, questioned the mob, and then allowed them to kick him more. I winced with every blow, for his body was emaciated and the offending feet were no doubt striking bone directly. When Bight deemed the punishment sufficient, he pulled the lad up, and looking at him squarely in the face, said, "Let zat be a lesson to you. Novone here gets avay with stealing. If I catch you again, it vill be I and not them who vill deal with you." The lad crumpled at Bight's feet when the large man let go of him. The mob dispersed and the lad was left in a heap, groaning. I am sure that at that moment he repented dearly for his sin, thankful that he was punished by the mob and not by Bight himself. I have seen the big man beat malefactors so badly that they died days later. But these deaths were overlooked by the Confederates. They treated Bight well and gave him and his associates more food than the rest of us.

Feb. 1st—Johnny Buehler died today. He was a young boy of seventeen with a face so cherubic as to preclude the thought that he enlisted to kill men. He was afflicted with scurvy and diarrhea, or quick step, as its called. We receive practically no fruits and vegetables, and as a result many are afflicted with scurvy. Johnny's teeth fell out and his face, by the time he died, had shriveled like a prune. He became somewhat attached to me, and when well, visited me often. I visited him when he could no longer move and lay prone by the diarrhea. Most of the prisoners have it. I am beginning to be affected. Such diseases come about for lack of nutrition. And what can we do with rotten and maggot-infested food? And the water from that stream is foul, but we are forced to drink it for thirst.

Johnny's head lay by my leg when he died. He could hardly talk, but he liked to listen to me speak of New York. He grew up there himself, but did not remember much of it. I was speaking to him and thought that he fell asleep. But he was dead. I helped move him to the pile of corpses that daily accumulate (there are about twenty each day). There was nothing I could do to prevent scavengers from taking his belongings.

Feb. 4th—Dreadfully cold. My hands are numb as I write. I can hardly feel them. If only there was a building where we could take shelter, for hole-filled tents are poor substitutes in this elemental arena. Part of the stream is frozen, and we must content ourselves with chunks of fetid ice.

Feb.8th—God save us. Don't let us perish so ignobly! Let me live to see my children again. They are both a year older now. Grant Frederick health to continue his duties. He is old. When Virginia returns with me, I shall give him retirement and a handsome pension. The old fellow deserves it. How well he has served me all of these years. Without him, our lives would not have been as comfortable.

Feb 13th—I was horribly ill for the last week, but now am better. I did not eat for many days because of diarrhea. As soon as I found I could move, I trekked to the stream and washed myself and my clothes. The cold water was tremendously refreshing and invigorating.

Not having any food, Kirby shared a piece of hoe-cake with me. He was proud of having made it. It had raisins in it and I do not know where he found them.

My tin cup was stolen. Perhaps while I lay sick some muggins came and took it. Woe is me now, for that tin cup has been very useful. How am I going to cook my food?

Feb.15th—I traded some buttons off my coat for a small, old pot. The pot has a hole on the side, and the water leaks out. I will try to find a plug for it today. But otherwise, it is a good pot.

Walking barefoot is not as much a hardship as I imagined. My feet have adjusted to the cold ground.

Feb.27th—We were let again outside the palisade to gather wood. There is such a dearth of wood within the stockade as to make life almost intolerable. I asked to go north of the stockade and was allowed to. There, while I gathered wood, I observed the layout of the grounds. There is a dense pine forest about a hundred yards north of the stockade. The kitchen is right by it. It felt very good to be outside, where the air is open and clean. The mass of unwashed bodies, and the general pollution, makes the air of the stockade unwholesome. I deliberated in my collecting, desiring to remain outside as long as possible. Merely being outside had a profound psychological effect on me. When I went back inside, my mind felt refreshed and hopeful. It is very easy to grow forlorn and despondent. The time outside remedied those feelings somewhat.

Mar. 4th—Virginia, pity me. I am so remorseful. How dared I lay a hand upon your person! How I love thee. I wish I was with thee.

> *Being your slave, what should I do but tend*
> *Upon the hours and times of your desire?*
> *I have no precious time at all to spend,*
> *Nor services to do, till you require.*

When I return to you, our roles will be reversed. I shall be your slave. Everything you ask for shall be yours.

Do you think of me? What an honor to be thought of. It is no small thing that one should spend the powers of mind on another. Do you think of me as I thought of Madeline? I mourn the loss of two women. Why God, did you form woman of man's rib, so close to his heart, so that the part there is left tender and injured. . .

Thus began a series of entries about Virginia. Perhaps my pitiful state conjured a pathos in me. My days became a continual worry because my physical condition had greatly deteriorated. My beard and hair were long and profuse; I was as thin as a lathe; and I walked about shoeless and in decrepitude. I knew that if Virginia saw me, she would so loathe me as to flee from my presence immediately.

Many men left behind wives and sweethearts. Some few had pictures of their darlings with them. They delighted in looking at them, as if the image was an almost perfect consolation for the actual presence. Alas, I had no image upon which to dote. I merely talked about Virginia, and in the ears of my listeners, she was transformed into a fair, golden-haired damsel. But in my heart she remained small and brown. This secret knowledge delighted me. When my friends pictured I courted a Venus, my mind dwelt upon my gentle Sheban queen.

Mar. 5th—I do not know what Virginia now thinks of me. Can it be that she loathes me? Has she not an ounce of compassion in her heart that has led her to forgive me? Have I not been good to her? I purchased her to give her freedom, and I loved her deeply. For a moment I failed her—but I did not hurt her. How could I hurt my gentle dove, who has fed me with her own hand? Virginia, forgive me, please. You do not know how I weep now. The tears lose themselves in my beard. My companions seek the reason for my lachrymosity. They think that I miss you. I do, and fear I have lost you. I meant you no wrong. Confusion overtook me. When I return I hope you allow me to make amends.

Mar.8th—There has been a recent attack by raiders and flankers. I have come to realize that they are a very organized group, like gypsies. Before I came, they murdered like Thugs. Now they confine their activities to pillaging. I curse them because they bring misery upon us. Do they not see that we are all in this hell together? But the scoundrels are selfish and worthless individuals, who would be about doing the same in society were they not confined to the stockade as prisoners of war. They took one poor fellow's blanket, right off his back as he slept. From another, at knife-point, they took a mirror and a valuable ring that had been in his family for generations. The scoundrels are hardly ever caught. But when they are, Bight deals with them.

Mar. 15th—The rumors of exchange are circulating again. Where they begin, I cannot guess. One fellow is so certain he will be exchanged, that he has packed up all of his belongings. For two nights he has slept in the open air with his meager articles around him. . .

Mar.16th—Several prisoners were exchanged today. What joy and excitement! The poor fellow from yesterday was left behind. He sits forlorn upon his articles. We have offered to help him rebuild his tent, but he waves us away.

Mar. 20th—Dreadful rains made my place muddy and unbearable. My tent was almost washed away. When the rain subsided, I was forced to find another station. The stockade stands on two hills, coming together in the valley through which the stream passes. The rains washed much filth and debris into the stream. I found there a ball of twine which sometime might be useful.

The stockade has been receiving prisoners every day and it is severely overcrowded. There is scarcely a square foot of ground that is not occupied. I moved to the northern section and thus a higher point, near the deadline. The inclined ground will protect me from wash-outs. There is an attenuation of prisoners as one gets nearer to the deadline.

Mar. 22nd—I had a dream last evening that left me somewhat shaken. I was in my house, playing with my children, when I heard Madeline call me from up the stairs. When I looked up, she stood on the top step. I called her down, but she refused to move. Instead she beckoned me to come up to her. But she did so without speaking, and yet I heard her distinctly. The more I begged her to descend, the more she pleaded I ascend. Does this mean my time is near? Part of me wishes it be so.

We received some oranges today, which, surprisingly, were fresh. I got one and bought two more from John Mosby. John was a sergeant in one of the Philadelphia regiments. His son served under him but was killed in the same action wherein he was captured. Poor man, there is not a day that passes that he does not speak of his son. He asks me why God did not take him instead. I could not answer. I feel like I am losing my faith. I cannot look at the horror that daily surrounds me; I cannot feel the hunger gnawing in my shrunken stomach; I cannot scrape my sores that have developed on my back, without doubting the benevolence of a sovereign Providence. The chaplain was exchanged; good for him. What of I and all the rest of these, many young lads who have experienced little else, their lives now being cut short by war?

Why is my pain perpetual,
And my wound incurable
Which refuses to be healed?
Will you surely be to me
Like an unreliable stream,
As waters that fail?

Oh, my faith was so strong, when I lived in ease and comfort, when my stomach was full, when my pockets were never wanting in gold, when my children played around me and my wife sat by my side. But surely the fire has been too strong. It has me burned up, even the dross. I feel bitter. God forgive my blasphemy. I believe; help my unbelief.

Mar. 26th—The guards atop the palisade are in plain view. I know them by name. One traded me two loaves of bread for one of my shiny buttons. I have four buttons on my coat left, and I shall continue to use them wisely. A few of the guards are very friendly to us and we talk with them and trade with them. They hug their muskets as they talk to us. We can only go up to the deadline and talk to them, but even then we do not get very close. Any transgression of the deadline means instant death. It is only a rope fence about twenty feet from the palisade, stretching from one side of the stockade to the other. I was told that some men purposely cross the deadline in order to be killed. They would rather die than continue in this misery.

Mar. 28th—An old man, Lieutenant Samuel Gumley, of the 6th Massachusetts, rushed over the deadline and was instantly shot through the heart. He lies there still, unmoved. He lost a leg to gangrene and recently became delirious, walking about as if possessed. I've had to shoo him away from me, and he hobbled away upon his crutch, mumbling nonsense. He hovered near the deadline, cursing the guards, and then tried to rush over it. He was killed immediately. We asked to remove his body, but the guards would not allow us to.

April 1st—Samuel Gumley's body remains. The guards want him there as an example. He is beginning to grow bloated, his once emaciated form seeming to gain some mass. The fools watch him, sometimes for hours. They bet whether a certain fly will enter his mouth. I do not watch him any longer. How much longer he will remain unburied, I do not know. But he should be allowed the dignity of a burial.

There are rumors that many prisoners will be exchanged. These rumors always abound. Some prisoners get what is called "exchange on the brain". They believe they will be exchanged soon and spend every moment anxious about it. I have seen men become so lifted in spirits about a rumor, that they simply died when the rumor did not materialize. I was affected with the disease once, such is my desire to leave this hellish place. I was even taken outside and put in line. But I was denied and sent back into the prison. I try now to keep my composure about the rumors, whether they be about exchange or about the propinquity of Federal troops. I must remain sane. I know so many men who are slightly insane. What else does a mind in a place like this become? I must continue writing and thinking of Virginia and my children. As soon as I get out, I will fetch Virginia. Then I will return home and be with my children. We will all be together. I wonder how they will accept Virginia. They will be taught to love her as I love her.

Virginia, how I need you. To hell with the estate. All I want is you. I need you to cut my hair and dress my sores, and to cook for me, and to read to me.

Why do I love you? Who taught me to love a slave? I do not know why I love you. If anybody knew the secret of my heart, what would they think?

I must remember what you look like. I must not forget. Caramel-colored, flawless skin; large brown eyes, tinged blue in the sunlight; hair like brown crepe, soft as gossamer. Your face is kindly and pleasant; the burdens you have carried through your life you have carefully hid. They have not mangled your lithe body, only given grace to your bearing. You have suffered greatly. Now I am tasting some of that suffering, not knowing how much longer I shall continue to taste it. We are one and the same now. Two wretched slaves.

But how I fear that I have offended you beyond condonation! What if I return and you do not wish to speak to me or see me? What if you do not love me? Do not tell me so, Virginia.....

After three months in the prison, I too became an emaciated, faded wraith. Had it not been for the green that was beginning to appear on the ground, I would have been an indistinguishable gray speck in a world of grayness. The clothes of the men, the tents, the ground, all commingled in leaden pallidity. We constantly walked about glassy-eyed, like hungry beasts, greatly fortunate when acquiring a piece of fruit, meat or vegetable.

An oven was finally built in the southwest corner of the stockade: a large, rectangular structure with metal shelves in long furnaces where bread could be baked. I tried to move near it, but found it impossible, the density of prisoners becoming unbearable. There must have been 30,000 men by the time the oven was built, in a prison that could comfortably hold perhaps a third of that.

We began to receive loaves of fresh bread several times a week, which was a boon to our nutrition. Because my stomach was fuller than it had been since I had arrived, and because the weather was warming, my spirits were generally lifted. I was able to awake from the wretched stupor that had kept me like a brute beast since I arrived. My mind began to work clearly again; I had new hopes. Shortly after I completed the above entry, I ceased to write in my journal altogether. The reason was that I became involved in a very interesting project, which, once accomplished, was to be the means to my freedom.

SEVENTEEN

MY SECOND ESCAPE

Since the time I arrived at Cahaba, a handful of men had tried to escape. Two men tried to flee while outside gathering wood. One was captured and the other was shot dead. Another man accomplished the feat of climbing over both palisades in the night. But he was also shot. There were also attempts at digging tunnels, but they ended in detection or failure.

While washing myself at the stream one day, I befriended an engineer attached to one of the Ohio regiments, Mede Butler. For whatever reason (perhaps he sensed something subversive about me) he began to confide in me his plan of digging a tunnel to escape the prison. It was dangerous to reveal such plans to none other than close companions. Many, for favor from the guards, often betrayed their friends.

I agreed to meet Mede that night at his tent near the eastern palisade. After wandering through the area for an hour, he saw me and hailed me, and I went to him. With him were two more men, a zouave from New York named Jim Walthall; and a young mute named Brian Thayer. Jim was wary of me when he saw me first, but Mede reassured him of my trustworthiness. We quickly became friends, and, before we even began our endeavor, were bonded in that way possible only under circumstances where men share a common distress.

Mede produced a sketch of the prison grounds, with approximations of the distances between the various buildings. Most of the structures, including the large pentagonal fort, the camp for the guards, and the officer's stockade, lay to the west. To the east there rose a series of earthworks, and, below the stream, the hospital buildings to which the sick went but hardly ever returned. Beyond was a pine and cypress forest extending to the Alabama river. The plan was to dig a tunnel so as to emerge beyond the earthworks, which would provide us some cover. The failures of past attempts at escape through tunneling were due to three reasons: treason, detection of the tunnel within the stockade, and detection once out of the stockade. One group inadvertently emerged near one of the guardhouses, were promptly apprehended, and sent back into the stockade. Of treason we had little fear, unless someone outside our company discovered us. To avoid the other problems, we worked very carefully, and only at night. We began to dig under Mede's tent with our bare hands a few hours every night, from midnight until three, conveying the earth in our shirts and hats to various areas so as to avoid any conspicuous accumulations. Diligently we tunneled until, by midsummer, we were clear of the palisades. The process took so long because our tunnels caved in repeatedly when we encountered sandy, rootless soil. We therefore had to redig many times until the passageway proved stable. We were always aware of the possibility of being buried alive, but our zeal to escape, and the claustrophobic nature of our work, compelled us to press on, without thought of danger.

Thought or no, the danger of a burial was real, and realized itself. The mute and I were underground digging while Mede and Jim conveyed the dirt out. A makeshift oil lamp we kept on the ground to illuminate our progress. Of a sudden, rose a grinding noise, and then a flurry of dust. The lamp fell dark and the tunnel became silent. Brian and I were confined to a small section, while the others were separated from us by several yards of soil. The poor mute was so terrified that he clung to me, cutting me with his nails, and emitting frightened moans. I was equally as terrified in that confined darkness. I began to dig from the walls when I realized that I had lost my orientation and was not at all sure in which direction lay my compatriots. They were to be found only in one direction; digging in any other would only produce a new tunnel and lead to nowhere. The only option was to dig upward; that direction, at least, I was certain of. I communicated my intention to Brian and we began scraping the ceiling, casting down handfuls of dirt and rocks upon our faces. Like madmen we dug, wary of causing another cave in from above. Were that to have occurred, we would surely have perished.

I estimated that a good eight feet of soil was still above us. I was sure of that estimate when we came upon roots, which was fortunate, for rooted ground is more compact and less likely to be dislodged en masse. Around the roots we dug until, two hours later, we were assailed by the cool night air.

We breathed it giddily, happy that the threat of asphyxiation was past. But I stayed the mute from continuing the last scrapes to our freedom when I remembered that we had not gone very far past the outer palisade, and that there existed a chance we would be spotted when emerging.

We left our pit carefully. The palisade was two hundred feet behind us. We could see the guards silhouetted atop it, their backs to us. On our hands and knees we slowly crawled a great distance, until, at my beckon, we sprang and ran for the forest like frightened deer. The blood was pounding so savagely in my ears that I heard nothing but it; and in the darkness I saw nothing, save the black mass of foliage ahead.

Across the field, the moon following, we ran, tripping over roots and troughs, bruising and cutting ourselves terribly. I tripped over a stump and fell headlong. I could hear Brian running ahead. But I also heard the dreadful sounds of the barking bloodhounds. "Run, Brian!" I cried as I pulled myself up and continued fleeing. But the poor lad, hearing poorly himself, heard neither me nor the dogs. He ran for his own sake.

Once in the forest, I knew not whither Brian had gone. I only knew that hounds and soldiers pursued me. Through the dark wood I proceeded cautiously, not wishing to clang my head against any low-hanging branches. But my caution did not prevent me from falling into a deep ravine. There the soldiers and their dogs found me, and like a dog myself, I was led back to the prison.

Brian was never caught. The lad, lame of tongue, was fleet of foot. Whether he made it North to freedom, or perished in a swamp, I can only guess. But it is my hope that as I write, he sits warmed by a fire, surrounded by kith and kin, and with the horrors of Cahaba only dim memories in his mind.

EIGHTEEN

WE TRY ANEW

One can only imagine that the guards made sport out of seeking fugitive prisoners, for neither I nor my two remaining comrades were subject to comeuppance, giving us incentive after a time to attempt our ploy again.

As soon as the weather cooled, our only indication of the coming of Fall, for there were no variegated leaves to alert us, we proceeded, being rather experienced already, to dig another tunnel. Another group, south of the stream, was also engaged in the same business, and we entered into a sort of competition as to who escaped first.

We began digging near the same entrance to our previous excavation, which we filled in under orders from the guards. But our destination remained the same: the earthworks. Mede decided not to allow any one else into our conspiracy, and so we three dug with the same diligence as when we were four.

It seems certain that had the authorities not built the ovens, to produce the bread, to feed more fully our wasted bodies, we would have never had the strength to undertake so arduous a project. It became especially difficult as winter set in, for the ground became unmalleable, and our progress hardgoing.

By the middle of December, our tunnel ran for more than seven hundred feet. The number is ambiguous. Some readers may be astounded that we tunneled for such a length; others disappointed that over such a long time so little progress was made. But it must be remembered that every inch of that soil was removed with bare hands and carried to various parts of the large space of the prison. That emaciated men, like human moles, could tunnel even a hundred feet, is worthy of recognition.

Mede, the engineer, true to his profession, judged that we were past the southernmost earthwork, and that it was time to dig upward. But, it being early morning when we reached that point, we decided to wait until nightfall. Merely crawling about on the outside, albeit under ground, proved a great satisfaction to each of us. We guarded the entrance to our freedom that day like eagles, and around midnight, plunged back into the darkness.

We took no lamp with us, shuffling slowly and blindly through every inch of those seven hundred feet. When we could go no further, with bowed heads, we dug upward. The first breath of air was to me more satisfying than the first time I attempted to escape. The stars twinkled mercifully above us. We were free.

As predicted, the earthwork was behind us, hiding part of the palisade from our view. We cautiously looked around for a sign of danger, but there was none. With an incredible, suppressed joy, we ran northeast toward a spur of pine. I spread my arms out as I ran, as if like a young bird, I was ready to fly.

We entered the wood with muffled cries of pain. The pine cones lay on the ground and hurt our bare feet. But we carried on, wanting to put as much distance between us and the prison. When we finally stopped, we lay on the ground panting, thankfully hearing only our deep breaths and not the sounds of our persecutors and their infernal canines. After a short rest we continued, this time walking briskly, for several hours.

We built a small fire and slept, as close as possible to the licking flames, until sunrise. In the morning we were all terribly hungry and became dismayed when it was discovered not one of us had bothered to pack a piece of bread. In addition, it was not known where we would be able to find food. The nearest places we knew of were Cahaba, and Selma, to the north. But traveling to either one of those places would have been like returning to the prison. We would be quickly spotted and apprehended.

The wood turned to a swamp as we neared the Alabama river, which was relatively calm. But it was too deep to ford at the point at which we came upon it, and so we went south a-ways until we could cross it. The water was unbearably cold on our bodies, but with grim faces we bore it, and reached the other side. We then scampered up the embankment to level ground, and continued our march.

As the sound of the Alabama attenuated behind us, we began to hear a singing voice. On our hands and knees we approached the source of the melody and came upon a negro, sitting on a log, polishing his axe. He sang:

> *Jesus call you, go in de wilderness,*
> *Go in de wilderness, go in de wilderness,*
> *Jesus call you, go in de wilderness*
> *To wait upon de Lawd.*
> *Go wait upon de Lawd,*
> *Go wait upon de Lawd,*
> *Go wait upon de Lawd, my God,*

He take away de sins ob de world.

Mede crawled up next to me.

"What do we do?" he asked. I looked at the negro, who seemed middle-aged: a hardened fellow, but apparently good-natured, and a possible ally. I stood.

"Hullo!" I yelled.

The negro was in the middle of "Go wait upon de Lawd" when he saw me. He was so frightened that he fell backwards behind the log. But in a second he was on his feet, axe ready.

"I ain't afeard ob ghosts en no men," he asserted. "If ye's a debil from hell, den, begone, I tells ye, in de name of Jesus!"

I, in my tattered clothes and disheveled hair, seemed no doubt like a fiend from hell. But I stepped forward.

"We mean you no harm," said I.

"Stay 'way from me!" the negro cried, brandishing his axe. "I don't care if ye's a debil. I'll cut ye down anyways."

"No!—please help us!" cried I. "We are men, escaped from the prison at Cahaba."

The negro looked at me inquisitively as I pulled up my two companions. Jim whispered in my ear, "He's prob'ly a fugitive slave. I hope he don't kill us with that axe."

"If ye's men, ye's look midy sorry," the negro said.

"We escaped yesterday from the prison," said I. "Can you help us find some food? We are terribly hungry."

The negro came closer to us, eyeballing us from top to bottom.

"Ye seems harmless 'nuff," he finally said. "Come wid me."

He led us downriver to a clearing, in the middle of which was a ramshackle log cabin. An old Labrador lay by the door, unmoving even at our presence. A negress came out of the cabin when we came in sight. She was tall and muscular, her long hair set in a sprouting of tightly wound tresses, like dormant serpents on the head of Medusa.

"Look wut I got!" he yelled to her.

"Who dey?" she responded alarmed.

"Dey's soljers. Union soljers."

"Dey look mo' like debils."

"Dat's what I thinks at fust. But dey's 'scaped from de prison."

The face of the negress brightened.

"Why, bless de Lawd, fo' de priblege ob helpin' Union soljers!" she intoned, kicked the dog out of the doorway, and opened the door wide for our admittance.

"Bring some chairs fo' dese soljers," the negress said to her husband. He rolled three polished stumps for us to sit on before their hearth. The negress brought out two blankets. One she gave to Jim. The other I shared with Mede.

"Dis here's my wife Lizzie," the negro, whose name was Isaac, said.

We introduced ourselves and told a bit of our extensive tunneling project. I was curious how they came to live in the wood and Isaac explained that he was a slave who escaped with his wife. They fled into the wood, and, undiscovered, made their home there.

"Dat was seben years 'go. I had my chance, and I took it, and I've been here eber since. Ain't that right, Lizzie?"

"We's been livin' here jes fine all dese years," Lizzie added. "As long as nobody come to git us, we'll do jes fine."

I felt terribly sorry for the precarious life these good people led. They were forced to flee and hide; but a mere twenty miles from a city like Selma, and so near to Cahaba, would they be safe forever? It was no matter that this man had built for himself a home, acquired his own food, had a wife. Were they to be found, none of that would be counted for him. He would be manacled with the bonds of slavery again, his home taken away, his wife separated from him. I then feared that our escape may have been detected after all. There were men who escaped from the prison only to be caught days or a week later. What if, because of the three of us, this poor family be detected? We, at worst, would be sent back to the prison. They—I shuddered to think it. I imagined Lizzie upon the auction block, fetching a high price, for she was proud, handsome in her maturity, stoutly built, of a chestnut complexion.

Lizzie cooked opossum for us, which we consumed with relish, despite the somewhat unwholesome taste.

"How's de war goin' on?" Isaac asked me.

"We don't know much, except that there is fighting in northern Alabama and that New Orleans is now under Union control."

"New Orleens?"

"Yes."

"When you think dey's coming up here? When dey come, we won't have to hide no mo'."

"I hope not."

"I hope dem soljers come soon."

I began to worry about the "soljers" again, and communicated my feelings to Mede and Jim. Mede agreed we were endangering the family and should leave immediately.

"But we've got t' figure out what we're going t' do now," Mede said.

"Do you know the area well?" I asked Isaac.

"Yes, sah, I do."

"What is around here?"

"Well, de wood goes for 'bout seben or eight miles dat way en dat. Dere ain't too many folks libin' 'round this place, 'cept po' folk."

"Selma is the nearest city?"

"'Suppose so, 'less dey bilt 'nother one in de pas' seben years."

In our zeal to escape, we did not consider what we were to do once we escaped. We were in the heart of the Confederacy, with Mississippi to our left and Georgia to our right. Above us we had two more slave states before we could reach free soil.

"We should remain in this forest," Jim observed. "If these niggers have lived here without being bothered for seven years, we can too, until the war is over. We can stay right here."

"I think—" I began but did not finish, interrupted by the Labrador who, suddenly coming to life, made a racket outside. Isaac sprung to the door, opened it, and saw the dog in a state of alert, looking toward the trees."

"What is it, Bones?"

The dog emitted a long, guttural growl, his eyes intent on the trees. We crowded at the entrance. Whatever alarmed the dog passed by us completely, for we stood as silently as possible listening for some abnormal noise. But there was nothing. . .until we began to discern the faintest barks, so faint that the point at which they were emitted was perhaps the farthest point they could originate with us barely hearing them.

"They're coming t' get us," Mede said. "They're comin' this way."

Isaac gave me a look of such helplessness that I despaired. Lizzie, who I took to be indestructible, filled with a stern pride, seemed to enervate in an instant. She addressed the three of us.

"You was followed?" she asked with despondent rage. "Why'd you come? How could you bring them here?"

"We did not know," I quickly said. "It seemed we escaped without detection. But there is no time to waste now. We must leave this place immediately."

"Oh, Lawd!" Lizzie began to weep. "How'se we gwyne to leeb our home? Dis here's all we got. I thought de fleeing days was ober. I don't want to go no place."

"But we got to go, Lizzie," Isaac said. "It was my fault for bringin' dem here. I didn' think det ef they 'scaped from de prison, de prison wuz gwyne to come after dem. But right now, dere ain't no time to be a-foolin'. We've got to go *now*."

"But where's we gwyne to go?"

"Well, I know where I'm'a going," Mede said, and stepped outside. "Come on, Jim, time to light out."

Jim also stepped outside.

"Aren't you coming with us?" Jim addressed me. I looked at them, and then at Lizzie. She stared at me with luminous, watery eyes. A compunction then bound me to my kind hosts. I could not leave them to share in my problem without me.

"It's best that we separate," I said. "You two go on. I'll stay with them."

Jim shook his head and turned to go. Mede said "So long!" to us and
followed. He turned one last time to thank Lizzie for the opossum.

We were certain now that the feeble barks heard before were real.
They echoed clearly through the wood. Lizzie ran through the cabin, which
was elemental in its rusticity, but which contained a domestic semblance to it
from the care of a woman, and collected certain important articles.

"Come on, Lizzie, hurry up!" Isaac pleaded.

"Oh, Lawd, my home!" Lizzie repeated and in another instant was
ready.

We left the cabin and I led them, without forethought, in the
direction of the river. My intention was to go south, and Isaac anticipated me.

"Soljer," he said, "dem debils got dogs, and dere ain't no way we's
gwyne to 'scape dem on foot. I got a raf' down de river a-ways dat we could
use. Good thing dem frends of yours went deyr own way 'cause dat raf' wud'a
been too small fo' all ob us."

Realizing we were heading in the same direction in which our pursuers
were coming, we hurried in fear, hoping that they were, at least, still on the
other side of the river. When we reached the gorge, we scanned the
embankment on the other side but saw no one; we only heard the dogs, so
clearly that they seemed almost on us. The descent was quite steep at this
point, causing Lizzie to slip and scrape herself on dried brambles. Once on the
bank, we ran for the raft, awash under a tree, a quarter of a mile down. But
before we reached it, we were sent scurrying by rifle shots from the top of the
opposite ridge. The bearings hit the water before us and raised the earth
behind us. I looked up and saw half a dozen guards, their rifles either trained
on us or in the process of being reloaded.

"Hi! You! Stop there!" we heard amidst the baying of the dogs, and followed by another volley of missiles. But, with no cover available, there was little we could do save reach the raft. Lizzie, Bones, and I jumped upon it, half of it in the water, while Isaac untied the tether. As the soldiers began to descend the slope, Isaac pushed out the raft, brought in the line, and we were bobbing down the river.

The soldiers set the dogs loose and they ran apace with us on the opposite bank, but the speed of the river conveyed us swiftly until all danger was left behind. Once we could hear no sound save the rushing of the water, we sighed in relief and lay back to rest out our fright and weariness.

NINETEEN

WE FLEE DOWN THE RIVER

Were this a work of fiction, the reader would perhaps accuse me of a contrived exaggeration in the telling of this tale. But I assure him that thus far all that I have related happened to me exactly as described, or as close as possible, allowing for a certain dimness of thought produced over time. And the story is not over still.

The raft measured eight feet by seven; it would have served us more comfortably had we been one less. I felt very odd in the presence of my hosts, for the circumstances under which we met, and by which we came to be together on a raft on the Alabama river, were less than desirable, and pointed above all to me as the culprit of the mess. Isaac, I could sense, perhaps out of pity for our common plight, had no rancor toward me. With him it was as if we had known each other a long time, and that we were sharing in one more escapade in a long line. Lizzie, on the other hand, was less than pleased at being forced from her home. At last, for perhaps the only time in her life, she had achieved a certain measure of peace and stability; and then, to have that all removed in a moment by an emaciated, dirty, stranger—a white man no less—must have been truly disheartening. She sat quietly on the forward corner of the raft, the dog beside her, when it had sufficiently lost its excitement and was still.

"Have you traveled far down the river?" I asked Isaac. He shook his head.

"Oh, no, soljer, neber far. I ont'ly clard de wood once o' twice. It ain't safe to clar de wood, no ways. Dere's houses 'long de river en dere's boats too on it. If ainbody sees me, deys gwyne to ask, 'Lookit dat nigger dar. What's he doin' alone on dat raf'? He must'a 'scaped frum some ware."

Lizzie suddenly interjected: "Isaac ain't I told you to not be using dat word? De buckra, dey's calls us niggers all dey like. But it ain't no good if we calls owlsel's niggers. Dere ain't no massah here no mo'."

"You'se rite, Lizzie, you'se rite. Wut you tol' me done left ma mind a second," Isaac apologized, and as he did so I was struck by her retort. Never had I heard a negro take offense at the word, whether spoken by white or black. The word is somewhat demeaning, said often patronizingly. But negroes use it amongst themselves quite freely. But it offended Lizzie, and I admired her conviction.

The river was wide enough around us to shield us from enemies on the shores, but boats on the water were a different matter. Being a white man, I could have prevaricated and told inquisitors that Isaac and Lizzie were my slaves. But how was I to be believed, looking as decrepit as I did, and without title or deed to my bondmen? Perhaps at another time we would have aroused less suspicion, but in the middle of a war over slavery, little latitude was given to abnormal situations. At the time I had no idea that President Lincoln had issued a preliminary proclamation of emancipation just three months before, giving the Confederate states one hundred days to give up the struggle without losing their slaves. There would have naturally been fears of insurrections and escapes. Fleeing negroes on a raft would not have been a comforting sight.

Still within the confine of the wood, Isaac grounded the raft and we left it to sit upon the ground. Lizzie's reticence made me very uncomfortable, the strain of which was broken only by Isaac's loquacity.

"Well, soljer, what we gwyne to do now?" he asked me. His epithet for me, perhaps inappropriate, seemed to fancy him, and so I left it to him.

"If I am not mistaken, this river flows straight into the Gulf," said I. "I am determined to reach New Orleans, which seems to me, presently, the nearest free area. As far as I know, no closer city or territory has yet been captured by the Union."

I began to address myself to Lizzie, who did not look at me, but only stared at the river: "I feel a deep regret that you and your husband were forced to leave your home. Truly, were it not for me and my companions, you would still be there at this moment in peaceful habitation. But fate has brought us together and has decreed that we be together a while longer. At this moment, I am as you, an outlaw and a fugitive. Were I to be caught, I would be sent back to prison or to some worse fate. With all the power that Providence has left me, I will try to secure your freedom. I have set my face toward New Orleans. If you come with me, there, you will truly be free."

I stopped speaking, hoping that my words would elicit some reaction from the negress. But she sat froward like before.

"We are still a long way off from Orleans," I continued, "and at this stage I do not see clearly how it is that we shall arrive there. But I pledge to you, on my honor, and by the eternal God, that I shall not betray you. Perhaps that is what you fear, for you both, being negroes, are in a greater danger than I."

"We'll be free in New Orleens, Lizzie," Isaac said excitedly. Lizzie turned her face to us for the first time. It was calm, almost fatuous, but I was overpowered by her stare. Some people not only have a certain distinctive character, they have it etched on their faces. Lizzie, in substance and demeanor, seemed like a rock, solid, defiant. She reminded me of Virginia in her unguarded moments, when her little face grew stern with determination, her eyebrows and lips working together to complete the image of resoluteness.

"We'll neber be free," she said simply and turned back to her former position. I swallowed hard, afraid that pronouncements more peremptory would leave her mouth.

As soon as nightfall came, we pushed off, desiring to clear the woods in the darkness. The night sky was only a narrow strip above us, bounded by tree tops, and the stars seemed to crowd in that little passage for our attention. But once we left the forest, the sky opened up in all its brilliance, and the stars twinkled at us incessantly from every direction.

The water rose to nearly ground level while we floated along most of the night. Occasionally a dark house would loom up, go past us, and disappear behind us. The river meandered greatly, going north for such a ways that I believed we were nearer to the prison than while in the forest. Thankfully, most of the area seemed unsettled and the banks were overgrown with trees and bushes.

Isaac and I divided the watch between us. When it was his turn to sleep, I sat aft with a plank ready, in case we drifted too far in one direction. Lizzie had not yet slept. She sat immovable to the side, huddled in a blanket, looking straight out into the snaky waterway. Bones, his golden coat silvery in the moonlight, lay quietly next to her.

Never in my life had I had the opportunity of so much interaction with negroes. Back home I knew only Frederick, and the handful of negroes I employed as laborers in my business. No doubt existed in my mind that the negro was a man as I, but there appeared to be clear differences in temperament and faculties. Except for those bred in a civilized environment, the negro seemed to me like a child in a man's body: without the capacity for logic or forethought, eager to please and loyal but impetuous—as Sam, superficially charming but lacking creative intelligence or substance. What future could millions of these, when freed, have in this white nation?

"Are you not tired?" I inquired of her gently. When silence was her answer, I said, "Please, do not hate me."

I decided not to pursue the matter any further, saddened that two women I had recently befriended grew to hate me, when I heard: "I don't hate you, soljer."

"But you are still angry with me." I said.

"I'm angry at many things," she said. "I taut I lef' all dat anger b'hind."

"It felt good to be free for a while."

"Good? It wuz hebenly. I'se been a slave all ma life, past from one fam'ly to de nex', from one fiel' to de nex', from one massah to de nex'. When I ran 'way wid my man, I couldn't beleeve it. Fo' once we didn' haf to be up by four to work in de fiel'. It wuz midy scary at de fust, 'cause we wasn't sho' if dey wuz gwyne to fin' us. But after a-while, nobody came an' we got used to being free. *Free*, ain't that sumting? Neber in my hole life would I a-thought it."

"I too tasted slavery," I said. "I was in that prison for a year."

"No, soljer, you didn'. Do' you were in dat pris'n, you were still free. I'd rader be a free man in a cal'boose that a slave in a fiel'. Yo' pris'n wuz walls, en you can clime ober de wall en 'scape, jes like you did. But my pris'n, I can't 'scape from it no matter how much I tries. All I kin do is haf faith in de Lawd, cause de Lawd, he looks down from heben, en he'll neber leave us or fo'sake us."

Several of the most horrible memories of my imprisonment then passed through my mind. Through my experience, I realized what those millions of poor innocents have been suffering for two centuries. That this *Christian* nation could produce a people so brutal and insensitive, pleased to enchain human beings and work them like pack animals, until their minds, bodies, and souls were gone, was a blight on the noble religion it espoused. And I, though never having set foot in the South until fate brought me thither, and who in word disdained slavery as immoral, was content to think the world must be as it must, and that any effort to change it would prove ineffectual. Sure, I thought this while sitting comfortably in my study, my face warmed by a cheerful fire, my wife and children sitting about me, my servant providing our every want. But cast me, as it happened, into the pit of abuse and injustice, misery and despair, and I begin to curse the world and its ways. This war suddenly became to me a glorious cause, and I wished the blue hordes to sweep over every inch of this cursed land to bring freedom and justice to the oppressed, and retribution to those who have crushed these people without whose aid I could never have survived my perils.

But what use was God to those who spent their last days eaten alive by vermin, watching their own flesh fester odiously? And what use was the Bible, or a few fragments of Scripture, clutched so tightly and reverently in the hand, to a man who was worn to the bone through starvation, and whose eyes were blind and teeth fallen out because of scurvy? Never once did I see Christ, so often on the lips of a dying man, save him; he died as wretchedly as the atheist. Yet the very men, nigh to the point of grievous death, clung to their God, their eyes fixed toward heaven, wide with a strange wonder, as if to them alone, in that last moment, were illuminated the glory and majesty of heaven. It is said that one can only truly know God through suffering. If that was the case, Lizzie must have known him intimately. I felt ashamed that my faith had so weakened through my trials. Lizzie was an example that the opposite was the nobler outcome.

"You love God, Lizzie?" I asked.

"Yes, wid all my hart. Don't you?"

I looked then at the dark, silvery water around me, heard the swish, swirl and lapping, felt the clean, cold air on my face, and realized that, for a time at least, I was safe. We were all safe. Our time was not yet over. Though we had been almost in the jaws of death, we were snatched from it. *Though a righteous man fall seven times, the Lord will lift him up.*

"I am trying to do so—again," I whispered, but I was sure that Lizzie did not hear me, for she remained silent. And for the rest of the night I quietly held the course, looking occasionally at the dark, huddled form before me, and beginning once again to thank Providence that we had not been forsaken utterly.

In the morning, we banked the raft in an envelope of willows and tall bulrushes, where a great amount of driftwood and trash had collected. About a mile downstream, on the left bank, we could see farm buildings. Throughout the night I had been thinking what next to do, and decided that it would be best if I at least found a way to make myself more presentable. The way I looked, inquisitors would be more suspicious of me than of the negroes. So I decided to take the chance of venturing ashore to see what I could find.

The place I left Isaac and Lizzie afforded sufficient cover. I promised to return as soon as possible, although I warned them that I might not be able to return for several days. But they were congenial to my plan, and offered to wait. Lizzie seemed more receptive; she was less taciturn. Before I left, she invoked a blessing for me, which I believe did more good than if a company of clerics had uttered it.

I jumped into the water and allowed the current to carry me for half the distance, striving to keep to the shore as much as possible, until I was able to swim to a convenient landing. Soaked, and looking like a wet, hirsute cat, I walked the rest of the way to the farm.

A rail fence surrounded a three-acre yard, and behind it a large house of hewed logs connected to what I took to be the kitchen and the smoke-house. To the other side of the kitchen stood several small cabins, a stable, and a mound of large, cotton bales. Beyond the fence were the fields, and in the distance, woods.

It was very quiet and still; and the leafless trees seemed ghostly with their drooping, finger-like branches. I climbed over the fence and walked slowly toward the house. A small dog tied to a horse post began to bark at me intermittently, as if it were not sure I was an intruder or an old friend of the family stopping by for a visit.

The front door of the house opened, and a dappled old hound came out, followed by a negro child of about seven. She stood upon the veranda in a tow-linen frock, and with the fingers of one hand in her mouth. I called to her gently, but she did not move. Presently the door opened again, and a negress wearing a colorful turban stepped out. As soon as she saw me, she pulled the child to her and held her protectively.

"What you want?" she hissed at me. I was a bit nervous myself, but decided to continue with what I had planned the night before should a situation like this arise.

"Pardon,—I was captured in battle and managed to escape," said I in the best Southern drawl I could create. "I've been floating down the river three days now, and just washed ashore. I'm terribly hungry and cold, and would appreciate some hospitality.

The negress seemed stunned. "A soljer from d'army? Why—" she began and then pulled the child into the house. The little dog continued to bark as I waited. The third time the door opened, a man in his forties came forth, short, but with broad shoulders, with a pipe protruding from his whiskers, followed by a woman and two young girls. The negress came forth last, without the negro child.

The man wasted no time, but came right up to me and looked me in the face.

"Lan' sakes, sir, where've you been?" he said, the pipe motionless in the corner of his mouth.

"There's been terrible fighting up a-ways," said I. "I've been afloat for three days now, and can't hardly take it no more."

I feigned to swoon and allowed the man to hold me up. He barked some orders to his "Missus" and to Joanne and Maryanne, his daughters. Even the negress put a hand in helping me up the steps to the porch, into the house, and up more steps to a bedroom. As they stripped away my rags and attired me in some clean linen, I acted delirious, exclaiming at proper intervals, "Long live the Confederacy!" or "Long live General Lee!" A bowl of delicious stew, real meat and potatoes, was brought to me, and it was the best meal I had had in a long time. I desired more, but I was so emaciated that the "Missus" feared

I would become ill. Finally, a cup of bitter liquid was given to me, and soon afterward my eyes closed upon the consoling sight of busy bodies hovering about me.

TWENTY

A REBEL ONCE MORE

It was the next day when I awoke, and my head throbbed with a painful ache. There was left for me, on a table by the bed, a small shaving mirror, a razor, and shears. On the bed, by my feet, lay a change of clothes: a sturdy cotton shirt and worsted breeches; on the floor a pair of worn shoes. I soon made use of the razor and shears. Once again I regained my smooth face, and my hair, a tangled jungle of growth, I reduced to a short and more becoming covering. The shirt was a slight bit too large, and the pants too short, but they accommodated me comfortably. The shoes fit remarkably well. After a destitute year at Cahaba, not even Solomon in all his glory was arrayed as I. Once finished, I felt and looked a new man, still thin from malnutrition, but new nevertheless.

I sat on the bed to think when the door opened and one of the daughters, I think it was Maryanne, a plump, good-natured girl of twelve, peeked her head in.

"Good afternoon," she said.

"Good afternoon," I said.

"You done slept for a day 'n a half."

"I didn't realize it had been that long."

"Every time I looked in, you was sleeping like a log."

"Where am I, exactly?"

"In my house."

"Yes," said I. "I mean, what's this area called?"

"Alabama," she said.

"Are there any towns near to here?"

"That're way is Biggsville."

Her father's voice now thundered from outside, "Maryanne, where're you? You better not be up in dar again. If you is, I'm gonna tan you!"

The girl looked behind her, afraid. "Got to go," she said, and ran. Presently, her father appeared. He saw the door opened and looked in.

"You didn't see my daughter 'round here, did you?" he asked.

"No," I said. "I just woke."

"Well, just as well. She's been stickin' her nose in here since we got you up. How'd you sleep?"

"Very well, thank you."

"You're lookin' better too. You looked like you been through a mill. My names's Orton Rufus, Ort for short. What's yours?"

"Mosby, John Mosby," I responded, taking the name of one of my fellow inmates at Cahaba.

"Mosby? You ain't from the Mosby's of Greenwood?"

"No, sir."

"Where're you from?"

"From?—good ol' Tennessee."

"Tennessee," he said dolefully. "I lost a boy at Shilo'. I lost my two good boys. I only got one left, an' I hope to God he's all right."

"I'm sorry."

"Well, you know how it is, Mosby. We got t'go out there an' fight for what we believe, to protect our land and prop'ty. I don't know what got into the heads of those damn Yankees, wantin' t'come down here where they don't b'long, an' disturb our lives, take our lands, our slaves, an' our sons. We never did nothing to 'em. Ain't that right?"

"Yes," I said, but beginning to feel ill at ease with my charade.

"I think they're just jalus, that's all. They don't like to see po' folk like me trying t'live in peace. I'm a hardworkin' man, Mosby, an' all I got I got with my own hands. Maybe I got slaves, but I'm right out with 'em most o' the time. I don't believe in having a body do somethin' for you that you can do yourself. Well, enuf o' this hokum. You must be hungrier than a bear out o' hibernin'. Come on with me an git some sup."

I followed him down the stairs to the dining table, at which was seated his wife and two daughters.

"This here's John Mosby," Orton introduced me. "He's from Tennessee, fightin' up at—where'd you tell me you was fightin'?"

"Up state a-ways," said I.

"It's a-comin' closer, then," he said. "We's proud t'have you here with us, John Mosby. May, he fought under—who'd you say you was fightin' under?"

"Piecemeal," I said quickly.

"Ah, yes, Piecemeal, I'd heard o' him. That's my wife May. My two girls are Maryanne and Joanne. Maryanne's the one who kept buttin' into your room."

"Sorry, Pa," Maryanne said contritely.

"Well, that's all right. I won't tan you," he said; then to me: "She's jus' 'cited, that's all."

They sat me at the head of the table. The servant came from the kitchen and filled the table with all things delightful: roast chicken, potatoes, turnips, butter-baked biscuits, bowls of apple and raspberry preserves, tender cauliflower, sweet corn, and hot apple cider. How I ate! No fare was ever as sumptuous. I thanked Providence with every bite, and blessed Him after every swallow.

"So how'd you 'scape?" Orton asked me.

"That's a long story. But I took to the river and clung to a piece of driftwood," I responded, intent on filling my belly. Let not the reader think I turned into a glutton, or that the purposes that had driven me thus far had somehow faded. I had not forgotten about Virginia, my children, or my friends on the raft. But when a man has not eaten a decent plateful in over a year, even his most noble aspirations are for a moment subjugated to the basic needs; and his roaring belly for a while overbears the silent ticking of his mind.

"Mr. Mosby, you think the fighting's gonna be reachin' us down here?" Orton's wife interrupted my feasting. "I'm afeard 'bout what's going to happen."

"I heard them Yanks'll burn down your house 'n take your niggers," Orton added.

"The last I heard" said I, "we were beating them."

"Hurrah for that!" Orton exclaimed, raising his cup of cider. "I'll drink to you, Mosby, and to th' army."

"And to Jed and Junior," his wife said.

"Yes, I musn't forget our boys," Orton said, a certain gravity in his voice. "They gave their lives brav'ly, to protect our home. They were both under Gen'ral Johnston. We got letters from the Gen'ral himself, telling us how brave our boys were. They died like men, Jed at Paducah, an' Ort Junior at Shilo'."

I heard a whimper and turned to see Orton's wife wiping her face with her napkin.

"Show 'im the letters, May," Orton instructed her. She left her chair, went to a secretary, and extracted from it a bundle of tissue. She unwrapped the letters and presented them to me. I looked them over and noticed the haphazard signature, placed there perhaps by some clerk in charge of mailing home letters to the families of the deceased. When I returned them, she wrapped them up carefully and returned them to the secretary.

"You kin stay here with us as long as you want, Mosby." Orton said to me. "A soldier of the Confed'racy we'll help any day."

Cups were again raised. All looked at me as if I had a nimbus about my head. They no doubt took me for some hero. Again I began to feel ill at ease, afraid that one of them would suddenly ask me to recount a battle story. Therefore I tried to change the subject.

"Mr. Rufus," I asked, "What do you grow on your farm?"

"Well, cotton, of course," he said. "I'm a small cotton farmer, is all. Got me only seven slaves, not counting Sophie, our house nigger, an' her daughter."

I noticed then, for the first time, that the child was sitting under the window, in a trough, her legs dangling over the rim. She had her finger in her mouth and eyed me complacently.

"You from a farm too?" Orton asked me.

"I—yes," I responded.

"You look like you got some shoolin' though."

"Yes," I began, but was cut short when Orton suddenly stood.

"Pardon me," he said, "but I got to call in the niggers."

With that he left the table. Sophie came and poured me more cider.

"Your daughter told me there was a town nearby," I said to Orton's wife.

"Yes—Biggsville," she said, "about ten miles."

"I would like to visit it in the morning, if I can."

"Surely, Ort kin take you."

The splendid meal was capped with a delicious cherry pie. By the time we finished, Orton came back. We retired to the sitting room and had scarcely taken our seats when we heard a knock at the door. Sophie emerged from the kitchen to answer it.

A man, wearing a large-brimmed hat, which he promptly removed, grinned in at us. Orton went to greet him.

"Good afternoon, Orton, Missus."

"Howdy, Duke, what brings you here?"

"Well, me and my brudder were skiffin' along the river when we came on the strangist sight. Are all your niggers in?"

"Why, I just called 'em in."

"You sure o' that?"

"Far as I know."

"'Cause me and my brudder, we found two niggers sitting on a raft, hiddin' in the willows 'bout a mile down."

When I heard that, my heart stopped and I sprang to Orton's side. The man stepped aside from the doorway.

"They b'long to you?" the man pointed his arm to the gate of the rail fence, at which another man was mounted on a rig. Behind him, their hands tied behind them, sat Isaac and Lizzie.

Orton peered out. "I reckon they're *not*."

"I didn't think they was."

"You found 'em on a raft? Well, they must've come from up river."

"That's what my brudder reckoned."

The man started for the rig and Orton followed. I remained within the house. When they reached it, the driver dismounted.

"They gave us hell of a fuss, 'specially the nigger gal," he said.

"She's a stout nigger, ain't she?"

"Yes, sir, she's good for the field."

"Did they say where they was from?"

"No, wouldn't speak a word. The nigger wanted t' say but the gal shut 'im up quick."

"Where're y'all from?" Orton asked them, but they were silent. "Up river a-ways, I bet. You don't b'long t' the Blakeses, do you?"

Isaac shook his head slightly.

"What're we going to do with 'em?" the man named Duke asked.

"You 'n your brudder better help me tie 'em up out back. I'll keep 'em here 'till we can find out who they b'long to."

They brought Isaac and Lizzie down from the rig, through the gate, and behind the house. I followed, trying not to be noticed, behind them, to see the men take them into a lean-to against the side of the stable. While they were inside, some of the slaves came out of their cabins to observe. Orton and the brothers emerged, and he secured a padlock on the door.

"They'll stay put 'till tomorrah," Orton said.

I made my way back to the house and went inside to wait. The brothers jumped on their rig and departed. Orton came in.

"Yep, same thing hap'end 'bout a month ago, ain't that right, May?"

"About a month," she agreed.

"We found a whole family o' fugitive niggers and kept 'em here. These are crazy times, with the war and Lincoln telling our niggers they's going t' be free. Niggers runnin' 'way right 'n left."

"What did you do with them?" I asked.

"Well, we kept 'em here a-while 'till we found they b'longed t' the Blakeses. But that nigger gal these boys found t'day is a mighty fine work nigger if I ever saw one. It's my Christen duty to return 'em to whoever they b'long to, but I hope I kin find some way t' keep 'er."

I did not say another word, so sick was I to the stomach. My gratuitous consumption perhaps had something to do with my gastric discomfort, but my concern for Isaac and Lizzie was the true culprit of my ailing.

Late that night, when I was sure the household was asleep, I slipped out of the house and headed for the lean-to. As I approached, a group of slaves, who had been crouching about the bottom of the door to the lean-to, looked up in fright and ran, disappearing into their cabins. When I reached the structure, I discovered that the bottom of the door was not level, affording a space of about a handsbreadth at its widest part. I kneeled down and put my mouth close to the opening.

"Issac? Lizzie?" I whispered.

"Who that?" I heard. "Soljer? Is't you?"

"It is I."

"I tol' you de soljer wuz gwyne t' come an help us," said Isaac.

"Now we're in a terrible fix," said I. "They are going to keep you here until it can be discovered who you belong to. If that fails, the master of the house may end up keeping you himself."

"You got t' get us out ob here, soljer," Lizzie said. "I don't want t' be a slave eber again."

"Yes, soljer, you got t' help us. We helped you, now you got t' help us."

"I know," said I without any idea how I was to do it. "But I ask for your patience. It may take a while for us to get out of this place. You'll be safe here, for the moment. Orton, the master of the house, does not seem to be too bad a fellow. He will not mistreat you."

"That's wut de niggers—um, de slaves—been telling us," Isaac said.

"I will try to look out for your well-being as much as possible. If they question you, you must not reveal any connection between us. They believe me to be a Confederate soldier. They must continue believing that or all is lost."

"Don't forgit us, soljer," Lizzie said with striking tenderness. I wished then to see her face.

"I shall not," said I, and went back to the house.

TWENTY-ONE

MEMORIES REKINDLED

On the first day of the new year, President Lincoln issued the Emancipation Proclamation, declaring that all slaves in those areas under Confederate control were to be forever free. The news reached us three days later, via the courier, who declared excitedly that slaves in large numbers were running off and crossing Union lines, or attaching themselves to approaching Union armies.

Orton wasted no time in assembling his slaves in the yard. Standing on a bench early one morning, he addressed them:

"By now y'all've heard 'bout that damned Lincoln's 'mancipatin' proclamatin'. Well, let me tell y'all right now, so that there's no mistakin', all that's a bunch o' hogwash. He's got no bizness down here no how, anyway. So don't let none of you git any hokey idears 'bout runnin 'way. You won't git very far 'fore I catch you. Now, y'all know I'm good to you, givin' you food, clothes, and homes t' live in for a good day's work. You know I don't 'spect nothin' more 'n that. But if you try t' double-cross me, thinkin' that you'se free an' whatnot, I'll send you to Biggsville straight an' no foolin'. I'll send you to the calaboose t' be whipped 'till you can't be whipped no mo'."

Ending his speech, he dispersed the slaves. I was sitting on the porch observing it all. Passing by me into the house, he grunted, "Damn that Lincoln, thinkin' he can 'mancipate *my* slaves!"

Over the next fortnight, Orton went into Biggsville often, I accompanying him, to check with the local constabulary concerning reports of any missing slaves fitting the descriptions of Isaac and Lizzie. He grew surer that no one would claim them, and happier because he desired to keep Lizzie for himself. I was surprised to discover that Pensacola had been under Union control since May of the previous year, and was closer to us even than New Orleans. Any chance of reaching New Orleans lay through Pensacola, which was much more accessible.

Isaac and Lizzie continued to be confined to the lean-to, but were well tended, for Sophie brought them two good meals a day; and the slaves, befriending them from the start, cared for further needs at night. I was able to persuade Orton to allow them to walk about outside, under my supervision, at least once a day, for the good of their health and circulation (for how could they work if they became unhealthy?). The dog Bones appeared one day, scratching at the fence. One of the girls allowed it to enter and it became an addition to the yard, resting often near the lean-to, to be close to its masters.

Returning one afternoon from walking with the negroes, and having the keys to the padlock of the lean-to and to the manacles by which their hands were bound, both of which Orton dutifully collected the second he saw me, I encountered a well-dressed gentleman sitting with Orton in the sitting room. I had my hand in my pocket, ready to return the keys, when Orton said to me,

"Come 'ere, Mosby. I'd like you t' meet a friend o' mine."

The gentleman stood to face me, with hand outstretched. I took it with a certain amiability when a memory stirred in my mind and tensed my whole body.

"This is Mr. W—", Orton said. "He's int'rested in buying one o' them niggers we found. An' this's John Mosby, from th'army. When we found 'im, he was sorry-lookin'. But two weeks here with the Missus, an' he's now fit as a fiddle."

"It is a pleasure," Mr. W— said to me. "You look somewhat familiar. Have we met before?"

I let go of his hand. Mr. W— was none other than the auctioneer from whom I had purchased Virginia.

"No, I don't think we have," I said.

"Have you ever been in New Orleans?"

"Never, sir," said I and sat down, trying very much to control the anger that was inside me when I remembered the horrible scene in which I saw Virginia for the first time. This was one of the men who abused my poor angel, and at that moment, I was powerless to do anything.

"Like I was sayin', Mr. W—," Orton said: "I'se been goin' t' town t' see if anybody done claim them niggers, but no body claims 'em. So I reckoned I kin keep 'em. There's two niggers, man 'n wife. I don't got no need for the nigger, but the nigger gal, I kin use her."

"How much would you be willing to give him up for?" Mr. W— asked.

"Well, I was thinkin', ma'be 2—"

"That sounds reasonable."

"Looks about forty, ma'be forty-five."

"You're going to sell Isaac?" I asked Orton.

"Yea, Mosby, if I kin git 2— for 'im."

"But you can't separate them."

"Why not?"

"Because they're man and wife."

"Don't you pay that no mind. You see, niggers is not like us folks. *They don't marry.* They thinks they git married, but it ain't so. One o' my niggers here, he got two wives, and Sophie's chile, that's his too. Now, you ain't going t' tell me that's marryin'? They're like animals, Mosby, don't you know?"

"But Orton, you simply cannot separate them. They have been together a long time."

"What a noble fellow!" Mr. W— said, pinching his chin and studying me closely.

"You'se takin' a likin' to them niggers Mosby?"

"I'll buy them both," I said.

"You got money?"

"Not with me—"

"Well, Mr. W—, he's got money *with* 'im, an' I ain't going t' argue no mo'. I don't know how you treat your niggers in Tennessee, Mosby, but down here we don't fuss much o'er 'em."

"I would like to see him before I make a decision," Mr. W— said.

"You kin see 'im now."

"I'll see him to-morrow. I've got some business in Biggsville now, but I'll be back this way to-morrow."

"I'll see you, then, Mr. W——."

Mr. W—— shook Orton's hand, then mine, his eyes still studying me. I feared that he would remember me and perhaps expose me in some fashion. But he left without a further word. Quickly, I feigned weariness and left Orton to retire to my room, feeling the keys in my pocket. There was no more time to waste. That very night we had to make our escape.

Again I waited until everyone was asleep to slip out of the house in the early hours with little more than the clothes on my back. I walked along the river road until I reached the envelope at which we first landed. Thankfully, the raft was still there, partly in the water. I climbed down to it, cleared away some of the debris that had accumulated around it, and pushed off on it. As I neared the house, I steered the raft close to the bank with the plank and grounded it.

The house was still dark as I returned to the yard, and the grounds quiet. With keys in hand, I made my way to the lean-to, before which lay Bones, awake but inert. I waved the dog away, inserted the key into the padlock, turned it carefully, and snapped it open. I heard a stirring inside, as if the inhabitants had just awakened.

"It is I," I whispered as I opened the door and went inside. It was so dark that I could not see the negroes. Knowing in what corner they were chained, I went there, but slipped on a tin plate, causing a considerable disturbance. When all was calm again, I felt for the manacles on their hands and unlocked them. As soon as I freed Lizzie, I felt her hands grab the sides of my head and pull me toward her. In the next instant I was smothered in such a kiss that I had to wipe my face with my shirt sleeve. As quietly as possible we headed toward the door. When I stepped outside, I was shocked, for in a semi-circle around the lean-to stood the slaves of the plantation. One of them whispered excitedly, "You'se gwyne to take us wid you?" In the next instant many of them fell on their knees pleading, "Please, sah, take us wid you. We wants to be free."

I feared that the noise would awake those in the house, and looked back anxiously at it. Lizzie then stepped forward, and with outstretched arm, like a queen commanding her vassals, she spoke:

"Lissen, now. We's going on a raf' that's too small eben fo' us. There ain't no way all ob you'se can come wid us. This here genelman is a soljer from de No'th, en he's been midy kind t' us. You all want to be free? I tells you, *you is already free 'cause ob what de Pres'dent say*. But it ain't gwyne t' do no good runnin' now, 'cause you gwyne t' be caught en sent to de cal'boose. De soljers'll come down soon 'nuff, en when dey come, den you can run to 'em. But fo' now you got to have longsuff'ring, en wait on de Lawd. I waited on de Lawd all my life, en he ain't neber fail me."

With those words the company of slaves was appeased. One old man stepped forward and said, "De Lawd be wid ye." I replaced the padlock on the door and headed toward the back of the yard, Lizzie, Isaac, and Bones following. As the company dispersed and went back to their cabins, a young, melodious voice sang softly,

> *We'll soon be free,*
> *We'll soon be free,*
> *We'll soon be free,*
> *When de Lawd will call us home.*

We followed the rail fence to the back gate and went out. Staying close to the fence, we walked all the way around toward the front of the plantation, crossed the road, reached the raft, and pushed off. In moments, the swift current took the house out of view, and we were once again alone under a blanket of stars.

TWENTY-TWO

THE PROMISED LAND

I instructed Isaac and Lizzie, were anyone to approach us, to sit quietly at the rear of the raft while I handled any inquiries. The night we left the Rufus plantation, we encountered nothing but a wall of timber to either side of us. By morning we began to pass houses and settlements. At one point we passed by a very large raft, almost three times the size of ours, with poles at each corner for lanterns, and huts in the center. There were four men visible, and one of them called out to me, asking if I knew how much sugar was selling for in Mobile. I responded that I had no idea, but was heading there myself. We glided near one another for a long time, until the current took our smaller raft past and away from the other.

I had little knowledge of the geography ahead of us, only that the next large city we would encounter would be Mobile. What a strange sensation I felt gliding down an unfamiliar waterway, heading where I knew not, ignorant of what perils still lay ahead. I was captain of my own small vessel, with a dog for a mascot, and Lizzie and Isaac for my first and second mates. New Orleans loomed in my mind like free soil in the mind of a toiling slave. It was somewhere there, a massive expanse of land unable to be missed, but still a long way off, and with many obstacles in its way.

The river entered another wooded area and descended into a deep gorge for a space, rock-imbedded cliffs looming precariously to each side of us, until it widened, and after a gradual fall, joined itself to another river, the Tombigree. The confluence of waters sent us spinning and cast us inconveniently toward the wrong side of the lip that separated the rivers. Through a valiant effort on all our parts, using the plank and our own hands, we were able to direct the raft toward what we thought was the continuing course of the Alabama, unsure where the Tombigree would take us, and wishing to continue heading toward a direction in which we were somewhat certain.

Not one of us had an idea how far Mobile still was. But to our surprise, scarcely ten leagues from the confluence, the land around us widened and we drifted into a small bay, guarded by innumerable seafowl which, upon flight, darkened the sky. Another league, and the water widened so considerably that it seemed, because of a dense mist shrouding the distance, that we were in open sea, with only the nearest shore accessible to us. And below us, on that shore, rose the waterside buildings of Mobile: the wharves, the sloops and large sailing vessels; and above the city, a grim fortification with canons like bristles out of a beast's hide. A line of floating canisters, torpedoes, dotted the bay, forming a protective barrier to the watery environs of the city. As we floated closer, the mists across the bay thinned and revealed another fortification, larger than the one by Mobile, with smooth embankments sloping up to a series of brick walls and ramparts. But the cynosure was a magnificent and improbable vessel—an ironclad warship—by itself at the entrance to a series of earthworks, like tiny fortified islands, that seemed one of the few entrance-ways to the city. It was a long submerged box, steel-plated with two turrets at the top, one fore and the larger mid-ship, embellished with a long gun protruding from a window. Men sat idly upon the deck, perhaps no longer amazed by the tempered Ark, while we, on our humble craft, were awed by the spectacular vessel.

We paddled with all our might to direct the raft to the left side of the bay, closest to Pensacola, where the great fort, which I later learned was named Fort Blakely, was situated. The floating mines and torpedoes were very numerous, and we steered around them, hoping that there were none hidden to our sight under the water. We wanted to land well away from the fort, but the current made it very difficult, bringing us ever closer to it, until we despaired that our landing would be in the face of a battery. But Providence gave us strength and we steered the raft toward the shore, about half a league above the fort, and in an area, desolate and overgrown, suitable to our covert work.

The embankment proved rocky and overgrown with brambles, causing us great hardship to reach level ground. Once we did, we grew disheartened that the land ahead of us was of similar topography. But we made our way as best as we could in a southwesterly direction, hoping to reach Pensacola, about fifty miles from where we landed, by late afternoon.

On the way, we feasted on the fig, banana, and orange trees we encountered, those which the frost allowed to keep some fruit, not having eaten since we left the plantation.

Our progress was momentarily halted by a river, through which we could find no convenient place to cross. But after walking downriver for a mile or two, we come to a narrow place spanned by a rope bridge. Once over, we walked for another two hours and arrived finally at Pensacola. It lay slightly below us, in a long valley fronted by the gulf. A fort on the bay towered over all of the other buildings. There was a section of the city, along the waterfront, that was destroyed by fire—buildings and warehouses left only to their skeletal frames.

We stood on the high ground a moment before continuing, looking at the city as if we had sought it all of our lives, and had finally found it. I thought then of Moses, how he must have felt standing alone upon the mount and beholding Canaan before him, the richest of all lands, flowing with sweet goodness, and knowing that he would not live to taste of it. Perhaps Isaac, beside me, was thinking the same, for in a sublime moment, with the sun setting fiery behind him, he stretched out an ashen finger and uttered passionately, "De Promis Lan'."

We descended first into a residential area. After a short time we came to a wide, busy avenue, where we fell upon a squad of Union soldiers on their way to some place. I came near one of the front officers and inquired where I could find his commander.

"Who wants t' know?" he asked dispassionately.

"Please, sir, I would like to speak with him," I entreated.

"It's Colonel Chapman," he said, looking first at me then at my companions walking behind me.

"Where can I find him?"

"His office is at the navy yard, at Wilson's saw mill."

"Thank you," said I, and left him to march on with his men.

"Where's dat?" Isaac asked me.

"It must be by the water," I responded, and proceeded in that direction, toward where many of the buildings had been burned down. When the Confederates evacuated the city, they were ordered to destroy it, particularly the important manufacturing establishments, the fort, and the boats. When the Union arrived, they succeeded in salvaging some of the torched property, but the fires had claimed a great deal.

We found Wilson's saw mill with the aid of a young negro, a slave recently escaped, who risked all and fled to Pensacola, living like a wild man in the wilderness until he found the city. Many slaves had done the same, for Pensacola was the only Union territory in a vast area, an island, like New Orleans, in a hostile sea.

The mill itself was partially scorched, but served as a garrison headquarters. Several soldiers standing guard outside challenged us, but I convinced them to let me see the Colonel. The negroes and their dog remained outside. I was led down to a cellar where I found Colonel Chapman, a thin, bearded man with clear blue eyes and a shock of tousled russet hair.

"Colonel, I have spent the last two years a prisoner at Cahaba," I began. "Having recently escaped at much peril, I am on my way back to my family and estate at New Orleans." Then I detailed some of the events from the beginning and of my unwilling enlistment into the Confederate army. The Colonel listened to my story with great surprise, marked by a tousling of his hair with his hand. When I was finished, he poured me a shot of whiskey from his canteen.

"That is the most remarkable tale I have ever heard," he said. "I am almost tempted to disregard everything you have told me, and to have you thrown out. But you seem like a very honorable and respectable fellow."

"Whether I am any of those things, I will not say. But I speak the truth. The negroes are outside and they can corroborate at least part of my story. You can also contact Mrs. Roget in Orleans."

"No need,—no need," he said, pouring me another shot. "I believe you. No one can invent a tale like that. You were made a captain, you say?"

"Yes, sir."

"Those secesh are desperate, aren't they? They'd as soon make Sherman commander of their army if they can buy him. Damn these rebels! When we arrived here, nearly a third of the place was destroyed. Ships, barracks, even the hospital. They lost more property at their own hands than they would have if they had given us a fight. They're going to be stuck with this place after we win the war, and there's no question of that, in my opinion."

"I need to get to New Orleans. Is there a vessel going in that direction some time soon?"

"Orleans, you say? You've got a big plantation there?"

"I would say medium-sized."

"How'd you like having slaves? I certainly have my share of niggers here. They're coming in from every God-forsaken nook of this land. You've got them coming in from Alabama, from Georgia, up from Florida. We've even had a few from the Carolinas. We've got to keep more of an eye on them sometimes than on the secesh still living in the city. Well, you're fortunate Orleans is in our hands. We'll be doing the same at Mobile soon. This whole coast will be ours, no question of it."

"I would like to get to Orleans as soon as I can."

"Sure, sure, don't you worry. We'll get you there. We got plenty of merchants who come from the islands, stop here, and then go over there. You'll be back there before you know it."

"My friends would like to remain here in the city if that is possible."

"Sure, they're welcome. Two more niggers won't make much of a difference. Did you know we've got colored regiments now?"

"I did not."

"My good friend Rufus Saxton had a hand in it. He's got a volunteer regiment in South Carolina. They're doing very well, I hear, on raids down the Georgia coast."

The Colonel would not allow me to go until he had found me a blue uniform. When I wore it, he decorated me with captain's stripes.

"You deserve it," he said to me. "Come around here to-morrow and we'll find you a means to go home. You can stay in the barracks tonight, if you wish."

With gratitude I left the Colonel, and dressed in my new outfit, returned to Isaac and Lizzie, who were waiting patiently outside, sitting on stacked wood planks, and with Bones lying quietly at their feet. When Lizzie saw me, she stood in front of me, and being as familiar with me as if we had been old friends, placed her hand on my shoulder and said "You look midy fine, soljer." Isaac readily agreed with the compliment and straightened out my hat.

"I will be leaving for the city to-morrow. You are welcomed to come with me."

"No," Lizzie said. "We've come to a good place, and we ain't movin' no mo'. Thank you, soljer, fo' helpin' us like you did. You risked yo' life fo' us, an' we's neber gwyne t' forgit it."

"Yes, sah, thank you much, sah," Isaac said with deep gratitude.

"I did nothing," I responded. "You bested me in faith and bravery."

"Wut eber you say, soljer," Lizzie said and embraced me. When she released me, Isaac came to me and took my hand warmly. They left me, their dog following, and I watched them go until I could see them no more. I only heard one solitary bark, as if Bones too contributed a farewell.

I did not have to wait until morning to leave Pensacola. A soldier came to tell me that a merchant ship, the *Rum Cake*, was leaving that very night from the navy yard, bound for New Orleans. I went to speak to the kindly captain, who readily agreed to transport me only if I joined him for dinner. That I did, in his cabin, with his first mate, and I entertained them with my adventures. By midnight, the *Rum Cake* left her dock and tacked against the wind into the lightless gulf. I slept not at all that night, but stayed on the fore deck looking out, eager to be the first to behold the city where my life had changed and where a dream still lingered.

TWENTY-THREE

ORLEANS

By morning we sailed smoothly through the misty network of islets at the tail of the Mississippi, and then past two masonry forts, like Scylla and Charybdis, that guarded the entrance to New Orleans. They stood grim on two promontories, gutted and battered, but with the welcoming flag of the United States floating above each. Confederate vessels lay scuttled by destroyed wharves, and another iron-clad lay still and silent, its armor dented and mangled on the starboard side. The Spring of the previous year, while I lay languishing at Cahaba, mortar shells burst and batteries spewed fire as Captain Farragut and his gun boats steamed up the river to capture the South's largest city. The fierce screams of battle had been silenced, but its reckless dissolution was evident on all sides.

The merchant ship docked and was immediately assailed by laborers, hungry for its cargo. I said farewell to the kind captain and left the *Rum Cake*, making my way through the maze of waterfront warehouses and other edifices, until I found myself on Fulton Street and in more familiar surroundings. The city looked very much the same as I had left it, except for the presence of Federal soldiers, as at Pensacola, standing in clusters by the major intersections. I also saw many more negroes than I did before; they sat in every doorway or milled about the streets. I searched around me for a soldier with a friendly countenance from whom I could ask the favor of finding me a carriage. I saw one standing by a shop. He had one foot on a porch step and was in conversation with a pretty young girl. Had not the girl brought me to his attention as I approached, he would not have noticed me, so engaged was he with her. But when he turned and recognized my rank, he stood at attention and saluted.

"At ease," said I to him. "Could you be so kind as to find me a carriage?"

"Yes, sir," said he and was about to go when the girl, who had been observing me with a marked curiosity, placed her hands to her mouth and excitedly cried, "Mr. Roget!"

"Oh David," she said to the soldier, jumping down to embrace me. "This is Mr. Roget. He's come home at last!"

I pulled her momentarily from me to examine her face. The pony tails were no more, their place taken by a handsome head of flavid locks. Her face had slendered and tanned, and had acquired that peculiar beauty that females achieve almost overnight on reaching maturity.

"Marguerite!—is it you?" said I, very happy to see her.

"Mr. Roget, look at you! You are so distinguished."

"Thank you," said I, choked by such an excited welcome to say much else.

"How we have missed you all of these years," she said. "When your letters stopped arriving we feared the worst. We thought you had perished. Mother tried to contact those officers that took you, but we never received a reply. This is the happiest day of my life! I prayed daily for your return, and here you are!"

The soldier finally put a word in. "This is the gentleman you always told me about?"

"The very one," Marguerite said.

"Captain," he said, "I'll get you your carriage."

When the carriage arrived, driven by a negro, Marguerite took my arm in hers and we boarded. With a tender blink to Marguerite and a salute to me, we left the soldier behind and were on our way through the streets of the city. After crossing the river, we traveled on the shelly river road toward the estate.

"And how is the family?" I inquired of Marguerite.

"Mother has been well, except when Thomas joined the army. She was terribly worried. But Thomas wanted to go so badly that as soon as he turned of age, he went off and joined. He's at Vicksburg now, guarding that place, and he writes often, so mother is no longer worried."

"A lad no more he is," said I. "He must be a handsome young man by now."

"Yes," Marguerite said, taking out a small photograph of Thomas in a gray uniform, looking out rather vacantly. But he had matured and looked a bit like I did at that age, resolute and thinking myself invincible.

"When the city was taken, mother feared that all of the slaves would abandon us, as occurred in many of the plantations around us. See that one there, Mr. Comstock's? It is in ruins now."

I saw the mansion pointed out to me. A dirty yellow had seeped over the white walls, most of its windows were smashed, and its garden was overgrown with weeds. The stately china trees that had adorned a walkway in front of the house had been cut down, and among its stumps scavenged a few dogs. A single negro sat on the veranda, rocking in a chair. He played a fiddle which sounded plaintively to my ears.

"But very few of our slaves—we call then hands now—left the house. Most of them remain still and work the land. Mother pays them wages, as you used to. As a result, we are still doing quite well, while the other plantations around us have fallen into ruin. Thank God that the city was peacefully taken, for the most part. The soldiers didn't come to destroy our homes, as I have heard was done on the coast. The Cushings, friends of my mother, lost their home in South Carolina. Negro soldiers pillaged the house and set fire to it, Mrs. Cushing told us. Isn't that a horror, to have negro soldiers? I have never seen one but I know that I would be scared of one. They already seem so ferocious as they are. What do you think of that, Mr. Roget?"

"I think they would make splendid soldiers, given what they have to fight for."

"I suppose. But please tell me, tell me all that has happened to you. Did you fight?"

"In one battle."

"Please tell me—I am dying to know. I am curious how it was that you left in gray and came back in blue."

I recounted to Marguerite some of my adventures, except that I withheld most of the horrible details of Cahaba, not wanting to offend her delicate sensitivity.

"And Sam?—where is Sam?"

"Sam was killed," said I and Marguerite became saddened.

"Poor Sam!" she lamented.   "And his child is grown and walking already."

The driver stopped the carriage on the road before the house as I directed. We dismounted and the carriage turned back slowly toward the city. A Union flag hung down over the entrance of the house from the central balcony. I walked slowly, Marguerite beside me, not wanting to miss an idyllic detail of what I considered, after much tribulation, my home. There were negro children in front of the house, as when I first arrived two years before. But the children had aged. What were babies then, stood waist high. What were lads and lasses then, were almost men and women. As we approached, they stopped their play and looked at us as if we were a supernatural sight.

I had not asked Marguerite about Virginia. A part of me desired to know nothing but her welfare. But another part wanted to know of her first by the sight of my eyes. I wanted not to hear of her; I wanted to behold her. I wanted then to take my African blossom and embrace her. My eyes scanned the grounds and buildings, as far as I could see, and every window of the house, for some sight of her. I guessed that she was in her room, napping on her lavender-scented sheets, dreaming of marigolds sparkling in the sunshine.

"Don't you know who this is?" Marguerite shouted to the children. "It's Master Roget!"

The children looked at one another. The older ones recognized me, while the younger ones seemed confused. They surrounded Marguerite and I as we climbed atop the veranda, putting out their hands and touching me as if they doubted my corporeality, mumbling greetings in surprised language. I patted their heads, recognizing or remembering only a few, and followed Marguerite into the house.

Marguerite ran first to the entrance of the parlor, crying, "Mother! Mother!" and then to the foot of the stairs. No one appeared but Deodra. She stood, mouth agape, and said, "Ma heavens!" I went to her, and despite my fear that she would be repulsed by me, placed my arms around her in a great embrace. She began to weep then, but grew afraid to do so on my shoulder. But I pushed her graying head toward it, and allowed her the pleasure.

Mrs. Roget appeared at the head of the stairs. When she saw me, she cried out my name and skipped down like an excited schoolgirl. It was the first time she had ever addressed me by my Christian name. It was in her arms next that I rested. Never did I see her, usually reserved in demeanor, display such warmth and emotion before.

"You should have seen the expression on my face, mother," Marguerite said, "when I saw him, out of the blue, walk up to us."

"We gave you up for dead," Mrs. Roget said to me. "I still cannot believe that you are here standing before me."

"I stand here not easily," said I. "I have told of some of my adventures to Marguerite—"

"Yes, Mother, what a time!"

"And I will divulge all in due time," said I. "But first tell me, have you heard anything of my children?"

"Of that," Mrs. Roget said, "you have nothing to worry. A year ago we began to receive mail again, and the letters from your servant dutifully arrived. Your children are well."

With that glad news, a great burden was lifted from me. Reader, if you are a father or mother, you will appreciate with what relief I learned that my daughters were safe and sound. My tribulations would not have been half as unbearable if I had known of the welfare of my children. I wished to see them at that moment; but unfortunately they were still a long way off.

"You must tell us all that has happened to you," Mrs. Roget said. "I am particularly intrigued how you left a Confederate and have come back a Yankee, an office that fits you better. But I see a great weariness in your eyes."

The excitement of events temporarily hid my weariness, but it must have been evident in my face nevertheless. Despite my objections to the contrary, tended by three gentle women, I was escorted up to my room and bedded. Deodra brought me some hot tea and laudanum. As I drank it, I thought of Virginia. The sedative was potent. In minutes I fell fast asleep.

TWENTY-FOUR

I FINALLY COMPREHEND

In the late afternoon I awoke, refreshed, and feeling quite well, although terribly hungry. Deodra came into the room to check on me, and finding me awake, bowed and was about to leave, when I called to her.

"How is Virginia?" I asked her.

Deodra looked away from me. "Virginny, sah?"

"Yes, is she in her room?"

"No, sah. She's preparin' supper."

With that she stepped out and closed the door. I left my bed, washed, shaved, and dressed for the meal.

When I entered the dining room, Mrs. Roget and Marguerite invited me to sit at my former place at the head of the table.

"It is good to have you dine with us, again, Mr. Roget," the mistress said. "Did you have a good rest?"

"A most satisfying one, thank you," I said, sitting down, keeping my eyes on the kitchen door, preparing myself for when it opened and Virginia should appear. Would she display joy at my return, or sorrow? I was afraid to look into her eyes, lest she condemn me with a scornful, or worse, indifferent expression. What was I to say to the saint I had venerated, and in whose faith I survived my travails?

"Why is not the wine on the table?" Mrs. Roget asked out loud. "Virginia! Please bring the wine."

I froze like a statue; such was my nervousness. The kitchen door opened and she appeared in an apron with a white kerchief around her head. She seemed not to have noticed me, for not once while she served wine to Marguerite and Mrs. Roget did she meet my gaze, so intent upon her handsome face. When it was my turn to be served, she kept her insouciant face lowered as she poured my wine.

"Virginia!" Mrs. Roget snapped with surprise. "Do you not remember who this is? Mr. Roget is back with us again."

Virginia's face then slowly lifted, and her dark eyes met mine. Though her face was calm, there seemed to be a perturbation in her eyes, as a mute who is burning to speak but without the wherewithal to do so. She seemed to look so deep within me that I felt her eyes scanning my inward parts, as if to find some reason or truth for my existence, some motive for my love, some compunction at my sins. Though I wanted to say something, though I wanted to reach out my arms and take this tender child within them, I could not. I was enervated by her powerful eyes, lights to a soul that was so pure and bright that it overshadowed even what I thought was my righteous, giving spirit.

"Welcome back, sir," she said simply and returned to the kitchen.

"What a strange girl!" Mrs. Roget remarked. "I am sure she has not forgotten what you did for her. Were I in her position, I would be jumping for joy to see you here."

Such a weight of sadness descended on me that I felt I was going to slump over my plate, or at the minimum, break into a torrent of tears. I regretted having returned, and wished I had perished in a battle, of starvation at Cahaba, or drowned in the river. Whatever joy I felt at my return dissipated completely at that moment. To be so coldly rejected by one I loved so dearly was the height of agony. And no one knew of it! The mistress and her daughter saw me outwardly, but knew nothing of the invisible knives that maimed me inside. What there was between Virginia and I was a secret; and my dejection was a secret also. Why not a smile, a glimmer of some hope for my hopes? What the trials of a hostile world could not do to my indomitable will, Virginia, in her humble disavowal, accomplished in a moment. I lost the love of one woman to death, and the other I killed to myself. All hope of reconciliation seemed lost. I had lost what first by mammon I brought, and then claimed by love.

"I think I shall return to my room to rest," said I.

"But you will not have supper?" Mrs. Roget asked.

"No," I said. "Please have Deodra bring up some tea."

I left and returned to my chamber, where I sat by the window and observed the stillness. All I could hear were the care-free shouts of children somewhere below me. When I was a child, I thought as a child; but when I became a man, I put away childish things. Oh, had I not been hasty in doing so! When I was a child, I knew nothing of the kind of sorrow I was experiencing. I never wept for one lost, or cried for a love betrayed. All my passions were in play, and from it gained my joy; and when sorrow, only for a moment, for someone was always there to comfort me.

Not another moment did I wish to linger in this place. I decided that as soon as possible, I would make arrangements to return to New York, if such was possible, to be with my daughters again. The plantation held up very well the time that I was gone, proof that I was not needed any longer there. My mission in the South, with much more than necessary added to it, seemed complete. To leave sorrow behind, it was necessary to leave the place of sorrow.

What was I thinking when I saw Virginia being auctioned away? Why did I buy her? I felt sorry for her, not wanting her to be given again into the hands of another abuser. But why did I love her? Was it merely her beauty? That, alone, was no reason to love. What kind of man would love a slave?— only one perhaps so lonely that he would give his affection to any woman who accepted it. Perhaps it was only an unnatural desire for dark flesh, said to possess Southern men. But no—it was not that. I had a genuine care for Virginia. I pitied her first, but then I loved her, wanting to make her, as alone as I, a part of my own family. I thought that she would love me also for my benevolence, the man who gave her freedom and the comforts of a home. But she did not love me, keeping herself from me from the beginning. Had I been wiser, I would have ended this game and allowed the situation to rest. But I saw her daily, and every time I did, she inflamed my passions like no woman has ever done. What was there in that bit of sable flesh that so stirred my heart? At first I thought it was a frail helplessness which aroused my paternalistic instincts. But then I came to see that it was quite the opposite; Virginia had no need for me. Her life in slavery had taught her to rely on herself. But she did not do so ostentatiously or rebelliously. In her quiet certitude she did more to fight her oppression than a hundred revolts would accomplish. I did not see that until I was buffeted myself, unable to control what happened to me. All that I could do was go forward, hoping that my situation would improve, but offering no surrender even to the kindness of men. Virginia, I knew not at all. I tried to take what was not mine, and failing, cursed the object instead of the weakness of my own heart.

A scream from outside startled me. It was followed by the frantic sound of a galloping horse. I craned my neck at the window, but could see nothing. Another scream echoed through the air, followed by the excited voices of people below. I stood to greet Deodra, who rushed into the room unable to speak from the exertion of running up the stairs. I grabbed her shoulders to steady her.

"What is it?" I declared disquietedly, affected by her own agitation.

"Virginny, sah," she cried, "he's took her!"

"What? Who took her?"

"Antoine Chevaux, sah, he done took her."

I looked toward the window and thought of the screams.

"Where, Deodra, where did he take her?"

"Don't know, sah, but they took off 'cross de field."

I rushed past her and ran downstairs to the parlor. Negroes were rushing in and out of the house. Marguerite stood weeping by the door. Mrs. Roget sat on the divan, her hand against her forehead. Her face, naturally pale, was a shade whiter. I sat by her and took her hand.

"He came in and threatened to kill me if I didn't let him in the pantry. He pushed me to the aside and took Virginia against her will. Oh, the horror!" Mrs. Roget cried, resting her head on my shoulder.

"But why do such a thing?" I asked.

"He had tried, repeatedly, to woo her while you were gone. But Virginia, peculiar girl as she is, always refused him. How strange, I thought, for they would have made a handsome couple. Now he has succeeded in taking her by force."

I looked up to see a ring of negroes staring worriedly at us. I immediately recognized Jubo and Cuba, who though waist-high lads when I left, had developed into stout and lusty youths.

"Did any of you see in what direction he headed?" I asked both. Jubo looked at Cuba, who began wringing his hands.

"I see's dem," Cuba said. "I wuz out back footin' de hoases and dey went that're way towad de bayou."

"I see's dem too," Jubo said, "though I cain't say which way they'se went 'cept that're way."

Jubo pointed toward the back corner of the parlor. Cuba pointed a slightly different way but adjusted his arm to match that of his companion.

"Cuba," I said, "saddle some horses for us. Jubo, find any firearms you can. We are going after them."

The lads' faces brightened with the expectation of an adventure. They scurried off in different directions. Mrs. Roget clutched my arm.

"Don't go, Stanton," she pleaded. "You'll be in danger."

"Not any more than I have been these years past," said I.

I was now consumed with a singular purpose: to rescue Virginia. I had prayed for a way to atone for the sin I had committed against her, and now the way was made clear for me to accomplish this purpose. Antoine Chevaux's actions now seemed entirely correspondent with his haughty, cruel nature. He was a man who had escaped the vicissitudes of a life normally ascribed to his race, and as a result felt that the world was his due. He looked on the fair Virginia as a prize, a laurel to complement the honorable station he had achieved. I should have recognized that he was capable of such a deed. He no doubt coveted Virginia from the moment he saw her. But did he know that I loved her? Was my sudden reappearance a threat to him? I marveled that the thought of Mr. Chevaux trying to court Virginia during my absence was not more prominent in the nightmares that had afflicted me during my tribulations. Virginia no doubt affected him like she did me—perhaps even more powerfully for nothing stood in his way except Virginia herself.

By the time I reached the stable, Jubo and Cuba had both accomplished their respective missions. Equipped with muskets, we took off at full gallop across the fields. With the sun hot on our faces, we were soon traversing a sea of roses, hyacinths and wild lilies. Led by Cuba, who seemed to know the lay of the land with comforting certitude, we proceeded toward the marshlands.

In time we were swallowed up by a hazy paradise of cypress and juniper trees whose dense, overarching foliage formed a new sky for us and only occasionally allowed us glimpses of the true luminous firmament. The sounds and smells were different than what I had ever experienced in other natural settings. Birds chirped and sang in divers melodies, exotic insects buzzed about our faces and the curious odor of springtime blossoms admixed with rotting wood suffused the atmosphere. The terrain was crisscrossed with watercourses, stretches of kelp and rushes, muddy bogs and ancient roots crawling like tentacles from the ground.

Our movement was slowed by the challenging terrain. We forded the rivulets with some difficulty, for the ground around them sucked at our horses' hooves like quicksand. Across a wide creek we espied a wooden shack, with access to it only by means of a rope bridge. Leaving the horses tied on one bank, we tested the bridge and crossed it slowly, afraid of falling into the terrible grips of alligators that rested peacefully below, only their eyes protruding through the algae patina of the water. Jubo explained that often times slaves, even before the city was captured, would escape and find refuge in these inhospitable swamps.

We approached the shack cautiously, which was no more than a single-room squarish structure built into the side of an eroded hillock. Had our quarry taken refuge there, we would have expected to see his horse tied nearby. But as such we saw nothing to suggest that it was occupied. There were no sounds or voices, either coming from inside; so confident, I pushed the door inward with the tip of my musket and stepped in when I realized that Cuba and Jubo stood mid-bridge observing me with looks of dismay on their faces. I directed my eyes to the object of their attention and saw they stared at a necklace of flowers and bits of bone that hung from an opening that served as a window.

"Sah, we'se betta git out 'o heah," Cuba said while Jubo swallowed hard and nodded in agreement.

"And why is that, Cuba?" I asked.

"That dere's the home ob a wich woman, Cuba said. "Wich woman's cass a spell on us en we die."

"That's utter nonsense," I said and continued through the door. But in an instant an old negress jumped in front of me and screamed something incomprehensible. I was shaken by the unexpected surprise and stumbled back out. Jubo and Cuba both turned on their heels and ran to the other side of the bridge in utter fright.

The old woman was of considerable girth, bent over and arrayed in a colorful headpiece and rags. One eye was glazed over in blindness. She wore a necklace similar to the one in the window and supported herself by means of a stout pole elaborately carved from a single branch.

The woman shouted at me in a strange tongue, although I was certain that solemn deprecations were part of her vocabulary. I looked back to Jubo and Cuba, who now safe on the other side of the creek, watched me with a certain relieved concern.

"What is she saying?" I shouted back to Cuba.

"She say we'se not welcome in de house," Cuba replied, "an that we'se betta git 'long quick."

I lowered my musket and raised my free hand in a peaceful gesture.

"Tell her we mean her no harm, that we're only looking for a man and a girl on horseback."

Cuba was silent for a moment and then responded in the foreign speech. The old woman directed her energy toward Jubo and responded vigorously. Both Jubo and Cuba cowered behind the horses. But when the old woman turned back to me, the expression of her furrowed, ancient face acquired a new, gentler cast.

"She say dey pass here, up de slope," Cuba translated for the old woman. "Two high-yaller niggers went on by de other side, up dere."

The old woman grabbed my shirt-sleeve and pulled me toward her as if to accentuate the importance of her message. She whispered something to me, but even the high, hurried pitch of her whisper carried clear across the creek.

"What was that, Jubo?" I demanded.

"She say the po' girl b'long to you sah, that you'se her massah, dat she don't b'long to de man she was wit," Jubo responded.

The old woman then smiled, placed a hand over my heart, and shuffled back into her hovel without another word.

Emboldened by what I interpreted was a fortuitous oracle, I ran across the bridge. My foot misstepped on a loose plankboard at one point, nearly making me dinner for the hungry alligators. Once on the other side, my two lads gave me an odd reception, for they remained behind the refuge of the horses.

"Come, men," I said, mounting my steed. "Let's make haste."

Cuba and Jubo sheepishly showed themselves, like children who are beckoned out of a hiding place after doing a misdeed.

"Sah, how'se you feelin'?" Jubo asked.

"Never better, my fine lad," said I. "I *am* under her spell."

My response elicited a plaintive cry from both the negroes.

"But worry not," I continued, "for such a spell quickens the heart and warms the soul."

With that I spurred my horse onward. My companions soon mounted and followed me, no doubt preferring the company of an accursed man to that of a mad witch-woman. The creek snaked through the morass with dizzying irregularity. Thick shrubbery concealed the presence of ruts which more than once caused our beasts to stumble. But we pressed on through the dreary bogs until we were arrested by another rivulet which joined the one we were paralleling. We were confronted, as it were, by a crossroads which at first examination offered no clue as to the true way to follow. I was about to proceed with the second watercourse as my guide when a gleam on the other side of it engaged my attention. Upon closer examination I discovered a woman's shoe half buried in the mud, it's metal eyelets betraying its position by reflecting the stray rays of sunlight. It took not long for me to realize that the shoe was of the pair I had purchased for Virginia the very day I acquired her! Again I succored my companions and we continued on the same course as before.

The light that penetrated the wetlands was waning, and I feared being caught in the bayou after dark since, in my haste, we neglected to take lanterns or torches. I was beginning even to doubt whether we had undertaken the correct route when agitated voices drifted toward us on the mists that now began to swirl about our stirruped feet. Ordering my companions to be silent, we dismounted and proceeded through a wall of tall brambles descending protectively toward a defile adjacent to the creek. On the other side, upon the log of a lightning-felled tree, sat Virginia. Antoine Chevaux, nearby, secured his exhausted mare. Virginia seemed in a daze, although her face showed evidence of much weeping.

Antoine attempted to take Virginia's hand, but she pulled it away as if it had touched something unclean. I was tempted to break into the clearing and confront my foe. Jubo, reading my thoughts, was eager to aid me. But I held myself and Jubo back, awaiting a better moment to act.

"We were meant for one another, *mademoiselle*," Antoine said, turning his back to Virginia and crossing his arms. "Yet you spurn me. Such cannot be."

"I do not love you," Virginia said, looking down to the ground with quivering lips.

"I, Antoine Marcel Chevaux, have always been a freedman. I call no one master but myself. You, however, were born a slave, and continue so."

"We are free now," Virginia retorted.

"Hah! Free, you say? Serving your mistress night and day is not freedom. And you have sat, pining away for *him*. For what? What more can he give you now?"

"He has given me everything already."

Antoine turned swiftly in anger, and seizing Virginia's arm said, "You speak as a child, *mademoiselle*. Our journey to the islands of my birth is yet long, and we have little time. But there we will marry and you shall be happy; you shall see."

"Unhand her!" I cried, jumping into the clearing. Jubo and Cuba followed me. Antoine relaxed his grip on Virginia and turned to me with steely composure.

"*Bâtard!*" he exclaimed. "But you are too late. I have claimed my reward for the long and faithful years I served under your father, who was a better man than you."

"You speak of reward, Mr. Chevaux, as if that fair blossom was a possession to be passed from hand to hand," I said. "There you are greatly mistaken."

"Were it truth or error, you shall not prevent me from having her," Antoine said.

I held my weapon at the ready. He glanced at it, and raising his hands, said, "I am unarmed, as you can see. Let us settle this as men—that is, unless you are afraid do so."

Feeling a bit foolish, and angry at his taunt, and giving in a bit to recklessness, I lowered my musket and signaled Jubo and Cuba to do the same. Antoine then walked toward me, rolling the sleeves of his shirt up his well-hewn forearms. I dropped the musket behind me and clenched my fists, instinctively raising them as a pugilist would, yet feeling a bit awkward at their positioning since I had never been in a serious fistfight. My lack of training soon proved itself. Antoine positioned his own fists in a much more elegant fashion, and before I could next blink, a set of knuckles broke through my defenses and, striking my jaw, felled me to the ground. He pulled me up to my feet and shoved me back, giving me another opportunity to be assailed. I shook my head to recollect my senses, and this time, raised an arm to prevent him from landing another blow on me. But he was as adept with his left hand as with his right, and struck me again with such power that I fell backward and lay in the dust as the world swam around me.

"What we do?—what we do?" cried Jubo and Cuba in anguished unison. I grasped my throbbing head with one hand and signaled again with the other that they should do nothing. I looked up to see the imposing overseer standing over me. He tried again to raise me, but I could not stand; the best I could do was to sit. Grasping me by the neck, he prepared his fist for what was to prove, no doubt, the final and decisive blow in this altercation; but then Virginia appeared beside us, and throwing herself on me to shield me, cried: "No Antoine! Do not hurt him any more!"

Antoine froze in a moment of indecision, then released me with a look of disgust. "This—this is what you want?" he asked Virginia, to which she replied in the affirmative with a trembling whisper. Without another word, Antoine walked calmly to his horse, mounted it, and rode out of the clearing, never to be seen again.

Fresh tears flowed from Virginia's eyes as she touched my bloody face.

"Stanton—" she began, but my face, also in tears, was so soon in her bosom that she silenced.

"That night I committed an injustice against you," I lamented. "The passions of my heart blinded me. Do you not understand how I feel for you?"

Virginia spoke in a whisper amidst her gentle sobs:

"How I have missed you, Stanton."

"You have?"

"Yes."

"Why, then, didn't you welcome me? Have you not forgiven me?"

"Stanton, it is you who must forgive me. I knew what you had to do, and so I kept myself, that you should not lose sight of who you are. There is nothing in me that you should desire. I was a slave, poor and wretched. My happiness would become your ruin. It was my hope that you would forget me; but when I looked into your eyes at supper, I knew that you had not. Please do not weep! You have not lost anything. You will go back home and forget me. It must be."

"No!—I came back for you! The very thought of you sustained me. I love you, Virginia. Don't you feel the same for me?"

"If I were to deny a love for my savior, for the man who has treated me with the most humane solicitude, I would deny all truth."

"Even when I—?"

"Speak of it no more. You did me no harm. I loved you from the moment you led me away from that evil crowd of men. When I sensed that you felt the same for me I dreamed—I'm ashamed by my brashness—that we would someday marry. But Stanton—oh, Stanton!—"

She could not continue, so strong were her emotions. I held her.

"Tell me."

"I'm ashamed to speak."

"Why?—do not be so with me."

"My former master—I was untruthful. He was not a good man."

"Oh! Virginia, my darling!"

"I thought—how could you ever love one as tainted and scarred as I?—" she faltered, weeping bitterly on my breast.

Images I'd rather soon forget passed through my mind as I imagined the abuse Virginia had suffered. The reasons for her reticence and shallowness grew clear to me in an illuminating instance. It was a deep and loathsome shame she felt, the painful embers of which reignited when I made my love to her known. How often does one, strapped with guilt, remove oneself from those who have it in their power to forgive and accept without question? One would rather continue in mortification than expose oneself to the possibility of further shame from those one loves. Love? Even in my present comfort there was no virtue for me in a kindness that may at first have only been sympathy, for according to the usual perversity of lovers, my desire was to receive more from her when everything had been taken from her already.

"Before I left," I said, "I swore to return, to take you with me, that where I go, there you may be also. You are going North with me."

I looked into her full and radiant face and said: "No longer as my servant—but as my wife."

Her demeanor changed, evident from minute alterations of her facial expressions: a widening of the eyes, an angulation of the eyebrows, slightly parted lips.

"Wife?" she whispered, short of breath. But before she could say aught else, I kissed her, and in that embrace two lonely, wounded souls lingered while Cuba and Jubo danced about us.

TWENTY-FIVE

HOME AGAIN

M rs. Roget, who was speechless when I brought Virginia back that day, later became rather disturbed when I told her of my intentions. She thought I had gone mad somewhere between the time I left and the time I arrived. Marguerite was delighted, having not lost her fondness for Virginia. And Deodra, that wise old woman, knew more about me than I, more about Virginia than she, and more of our relationship than we did. She promised me that, for the ceremony, she was going to transform Virginia into the most beautiful young lady who ever gave her hand in matrimony. I told her that to improve on perfection was truly a most difficult endeavor.

We succeeded in finding a parson who scrupled not at performing the ceremony, if only because a rather large stipend blinded him to the unlawfulness of miscegenation. The following month, Virginia and I were married in a private ceremony. By private I mean our own household; and by household I mean all who lived on the plantation. In order not to cause Mrs. Roget undue grief by having four dozen negroes, besides rambunctious children, stomping through the house, we held the wedding in the large cabin used by the negroes as a dining hall. There, all could exist comfortably, and the negroes could dance all that they wanted. And dance they did! Whether out of happiness for Virginia and I, or from the fact that I supplied all of the spirits they desired, the negroes enjoyed quite a celebration. Even Mary, for weeks rapt with grief, seemed to enjoy herself, with her little son on her lap, in the company of many of the negro women.

Jubo, a fine-looking lad once scrubbed and dressed in a new suit, which I gave him to keep, to his joy, served as my ring-bearer. But the cynosure in that rustic log house, under the wavy lights of a dozen lanterns, the apple of mine and every dusky eye there, was Virginia, dressed marvelously in a white muslin gown hemmed with pink silk gallons, and a flower studded bonnet with a gossamer veil. I forgot everything that had ever happened to me when I saw that handsome mulatto, so finely dressed in pearly radiance; and when I lifted the veil and beheld that roseate, creamy face so full of love and gratitude, time and the world stopped. If Providence, at the end of such an arduous road, brought one to such great joy, I wished to be passed through greater fires.

It was not until July that Virginia and I were able to leave New Orleans, for until then Vicksburg had been under Confederate control. But a siege of the city by Major-General Grant, begun in late May and lasting until early July, opened access to the Mississippi north of Vicksburg. Thomas, wounded in the struggle, was sent home and we were happy to receive him.

It was quite a wait for me, not knowing when we would be free to travel. So as soon as news arrived of Grant's victory, and as soon as steam boat companies began operating again, we reserved our place and went our way, leaving the plantation in the capable hands of the faithful negroes. Before leaving, with Mrs. Roget's permission, the land was divided into plots so that individual negroes and families, like sharecroppers, would have some soil which they could tend. They abandoned their cabins and built homes of their own throughout the fields, clearing the cane for small homesteads. Since the negroes were free, I believed that the estate would be best run by a sharecropping system. The same was done throughout the South after the war, during the period of Reconstruction, but with much less success for the unfortunate negroes. Their conditions improved little from the slavery of before. But such was not the case with my plantation, for Mrs. Roget was an equitable woman, and the negroes lived well as long as they profited the estate.

We arrived in New York City in the wake of terrible riots in response to the conscription act passed by the government. About a hundred persons, many of them negroes, were killed. The city was still in a state of alarm the morning Virginia and I arrived at the station, and I had to dutifully explain to her that the city, despite its lurid reputation, was a quite a safe place; we had only arrived at an unusual moment.

Virginia was delighted by the verdure of my home's environs. The maple and hickory trees of Inwood stood tall and vibrant around us, their leaves forming a canopy over the road on which we traveled. The forest opened to my humble homestead, where an abundant assortment of flowers grew wildly, orchids and red marigolds, gaping petunias and sleeping four o'clocks, zinnias and bignonias. The variegation at the time of year was tremendous, and Virginia stared in marvel at the botanical garden in which I made my home.

Approaching the house, I could see my children playing in the yard. Having the opportunity to observe them before they did me, I looked with excitement at my two girls. They had both grown somewhat the time that I was gone, and my little Andrea was not so little any longer. They delighted in play, running about, their summer dresses flapping in the wind.

I asked the driver to stop the cab, and stepped out, leaving Virginia inside. Andrea was the first to stop her play, and stood still watching me approach. Madeline turned to see what was the matter, and immediately shouted out "Poppa!" The two girls then ran into my waiting arms, to embrace a heaving chest, wherein we shared a torrent of tears and kisses.

"Look, dear daughters, I have brought with me someone very special," said I, and then called Virginia. She stepped out, looking sheepish, in the florid damask dress I had brought her for the homecoming.

"This is Virginia—Virginia Roget, my new wife, and your new step-mother."

Andrea, never bashful of strangers, went up to Virginia, curtsied very lady-like, and said, "Pleased to meet you." Virginia picked up her skirt, curtsied, and said, "I have heard much about you, Andrea."

Madeline tugged at my arm, and in a whisper began, "Poppa. . ." but I stopped her, knowing that it would still take some while for her to become accustomed to someone new in the house, a new wife and step-mother, a shade darker than herself.

Frederick met us at the door, and after weeping on my neck, kissed many times the hands of Virginia. Then he worriedly informed me that draft officers had made a call at the house several days before. I told him not to be concerned, that I had seen both sides of the conflict, and wearied of it, would not allow myself to be moved anywhere again. I wanted to be no place but home, with my wife and children—my family, the one constant joy life allows us.

In Virginia I found the same virtuous soul as Madeline's, the same nobleness, the same maternalism. Providence could not have blessed me with a more lovely helpmeet, diligent in the service of her family, munificent in kindness, honest and loyal.

What need is there more to say? I hasten now to end this narrative;

one, by an old merchant and soldier whose children have grown and gone to travel on their own paths. Virginia, perhaps no longer a blossom, but still the flower of my eyes, remembers those days, when servitude was the law of her land and the bane of her people, when she served night and day, bound by invisible chains, with quiet disbelief. The world has changed greatly since then, and we are glad we have changed with it; but not our love, the most beautiful of all frustrations, for it remains more than can ever be expressed.

About the Author

Richard Bertematti was educated at Trinity School in Manhattan and Northwestern University.

Visit www.bertematti.com